SHELV~~ED~~
FOR M~~URDER~~

"Has there been an accident?"

"The janitor . . . Jack, you know . . . found a body when he came in this morning. A dead body."

"Where?" she asked.

"In the stacks."

"Was it . . . murder?"

"The police think he was killed after the library closed last night."

"Fiction or nonfiction?"

Mr. Upman took his hands from his face and considered Helma sternly. "I'm not making it up," he said indignantly.

"No, was the body in the fiction or nonfiction stacks?"

Mr. Upman shrugged. "Fiction stacks. In the MO-NE aisle, I think."

In the stacks, men in plain suits, but with an undefinable authoritative bearing, prodded among the books and squinted along the window ledges.

Murder. Murder in the library.

MISS ZUKAS
✺ AND THE ✺
LIBRARY MURDERS

✺ JO DERESKE ✺

AVON BOOKS  NEW YORK

For June Dereske

MISS ZUKAS AND THE LIBRARY MURDERS is an original publication of Avon Books. This work has never before appeared in book form. This work is a novel. Any similarity to actual persons or events is purely coincidental.

AVON BOOKS
A division of
The Hearst Corporation
1350 Avenue of the Americas
New York, New York 10019

Copyright © 1994 by Jo Dereske
Published by arrangement with the author
Library of Congress Catalog Card Number: 93-90641
ISBN: 0-380-77030-X

First Avon Books Printing: March 1994

AVON TRADEMARK REG. U.S. PAT. OFF. AND IN OTHER COUNTRIES, MARCA REGISTRADA, HECHO EN U.S.A.

Printed in the U.S.A.

RA   10 9 8 7 6 5 4 3 2 1

CONTENTS

chapter one

THE BODY IN THE FICTION AISLE

On Thursday morning, when Jack the janitor stumbled over the body in the Mo–Ne aisle of the fiction stacks, losing his oatmeal and orange juice only a little way from the outreaching shadow of dark blood, Miss Helma Zukas was late for work, a rare occurrence that caused her to miss the initial hysteria and excitement of the discovery.

Miss Zukas was just sliding behind the wheel of her Buick, dressed for a day at the public library, all except for the brown oxfords she wore to and from work to save her heels, when she glanced out over Washington Bay and saw sunlight glimmering through the cement gray clouds. Golden beams flickered wanly on the distant crown of Orcas Island. But it was enough of a warning for Helma. She was certain she hadn't pulled down the opaque shades that protected her furnishings from the sun.

"I should have known this weather couldn't last," she said to herself as she climbed the outside stairs to the third floor of the Bayside Arms, avoiding the elevator because Miss Zukas always avoided elevators. She was going to be late for work, but it couldn't be helped.

1

The Bayside Arms stood on a bank above Washington Bay, three stories tall and holding eighteen apartments. Except for its location, the Bayside Arms was unexceptional, unadorned by architectural embellishment, neatly painted, and tidily maintained. The side of the building facing the parking lot and street was strung with outside landings like a motel. Small balconies jutted from each apartment on the opposite side, facing the bay. Helma's apartment was second from the end on the third floor.

As was her habit, Helma swept a quick eye around her apartment as she entered. All was in order and yes, she *had* left the shades up.

Light sparkled off the water and the day definitely threatened sunshine. Helma unrolled the plastic shades on her picture window and the sliding glass door that led out to her small balcony. Her apartment slipped into a twilight of soft shadows.

Helma Zukas had moved into apartment 3F when the Bayside Arms first opened fourteen years earlier. At that time, she was a fresh library school graduate from Michigan and had just arrived in Washington state to accept her position at the Bellehaven Public Library. It was her first trip out of Michigan and 3F was the first place she'd ever lived that belonged only to her.

There were two bedrooms in Miss Zukas's apartment. Her own, which was done in beige-pinks, like the rest of her apartment, and a guest bedroom, which she referred to as "the back bedroom," where she also kept gifts which didn't suit her tastes, but which had been given to her by people whose feelings she couldn't bear to hurt. Among other items in the back bedroom was an intricate Indian blanket on the guest bed—a gift from her mother—and a small, too-bright painting done by her friend Ruth. When she didn't have guests, Helma kept the door of the back bedroom closed.

All the paintings on Miss Zukas's walls were originals done in the school of realism: pleasant beige land-scapes; pastel still lifes; gleaming white sailboats on tame seas.

Aside from a barely noticeable stain on the beige carpet where her friend Ruth had spilled a cup of coffee one night when Helma was trying to sober her up, Helma's apartment was in as pristine shape as it had been fourteen years ago when she carried in her first labeled cardboard box of kitchen cutlery.

She turned to leave, glancing at her watch and noting she was already five minutes late. Her foot caught on the dish under her Chinese elm and the ceramic pot tipped onto the carpet, spilling a cascade of black dirt across the rug.

"Oh, Faulkner!" she said through tight lips, kneeling to right the plant and scoop up the dirt with her hands. It would take at least fifteen minutes to get every bit of it out of the carpet. This called for her vacuum, and the spot remover, too.

She sighed and stood, holding her dirt-covered hands in front of her, away from her skirt.

Bellehaven sat on the edge of calm waters, protected from the moods of the Pacific Ocean by Washington Bay and the San Juan Islands. Behind the city, the land rose upward into the foothills and then the snow-covered and jagged Cascade range that blocked the easterly progress of rain clouds, forcing them to release their wet burden on Bellehaven's side of the mountains. Rain and gray skies and misty vistas were frequent in Bellehaven and a period of weeks without sunshine wasn't unusual. Because of this, Bellehaven was temperate year round: lush, succulent, a gardener's paradise, although sunflowers were as uncommon as suntans.

The public library, the city hall, the courthouse, and the police station, all built of similar brick architecture, occupied one oversize block in downtown Bellehaven.

The rectangular brick library was one of a universal design popular in the no-frills sixties: flat-roofed, recessed windows, plate glass doors, a tendency to huddle close to the earth.

It wasn't unusual for the police to park near the library, but when Helma pulled her Buick into the tiny library lot, a black-and-white police car was parked in her space. A gibberish of police radio static buzzed out through its open windows. There were only six parking spaces and twenty library employees; Helma had had to wait four years for her own parking slot, and after ten years she considered it her personal property.

She studied the police car for a few moments, bit her lip, and parked her own Buick crosswise behind it.

Helma worked at the Bellehaven Public Library five days a week and one Saturday a month. She had five weeks of paid vacation a year because she'd been employed by the library for fourteen years and it was the maximum paid vacation allotted to a city employee. She'd also accumulated 166 days of paid sick leave, the most unused sick days on record.

She liked her job and realistically knew she was very good at it. If a patron asked her a question she couldn't answer, Helma took his or her name and number and phoned when she did have the answer, no matter how long it took. Once a woman had asked coyly if there were boy slugs and girl slugs. Six months later Helma found the answer while she was reading a book of Northwest trivia and phoned the woman, who still didn't know: there weren't.

Helma stopped and blinked her eyes. An ambulance was backed up to the book ramp where the bookmobile usually parked. Its rear doors gaped open but at least its lights weren't gyrating, so Helma didn't think there could be a life-threatening emergency in the library. A young policeman stood on the ramp next to the staff entrance, calmly watching Helma's approach, his arms at his sides, his gun in place.

He's standing guard, she thought to herself, and a not-unpleasant thrill of dread prickled along the back of her neck.

"May I see some identification?" he asked politely, touching the brim of his cap.

Miss Zukas rarely raised her voice beyond a conversational level. Instead, when necessary, she had perfected a chilling calmness to her speech, like silver dimes dropping into ice water. It worked wonders on anyone who had ever been a child.

"What is the meaning of this?" Helma asked.

The policeman faltered for the briefest moment and a look of uncertainty passed across his eyes.

"I'm sorry," he replied apologetically but firmly, standing steadfast, "but do you have a right to be in this building?"

The staff door swung open and Mr. Upman, the library director, hurried forward, one hand raised like a traffic director stopping traffic. The knot of his paisley tie was twisted to the left of center.

"It's all right, officer. She's one of us. Good morning, Miss Zukas."

"I'm not certain it does look like a very good morning," Miss Zukas told Mr. Upman.

He nodded, bobbing his head, and beckoned Helma inside. The furrows in his forehead rippled, merging into his shiny bald scalp. Steam dotted the upper corners of his glasses.

As Helma passed Mr. Upman, he placed his hand on her elbow. She sidestepped until he had to drop his hand or reach foolishly far.

Mr. Upman was fiftyish; it showed on his face. But Helma had driven past him once as he jogged along the sidewalk in bright blue shorts and a white T-shirt. She'd been so astonished that a muscled body, as tight and trim as a gymnast's, coexisted with his pallid, bald, myopic head that for a moment she'd forgotten herself and blatantly stared.

Mr. Upman dropped his hand, a flush of red rising in his cheeks. He liked to touch. Rumors had it that . . . but then Helma didn't like to listen to rumors.

The cramped workroom, normally bustling with library business, was empty. The purple nylon bag Eve called her purse sat out on her desk next to her stuffed Paddington Bear. Patrice's tailored coat was draped over the back of her chair. Helma didn't smell any coffee.

"There is a police car in my parking space," Helma informed Mr. Upman. "And why is there an ambulance parked at the book ramp? Not to mention a policeman at the door?"

He nodded distractedly and folded his hands together over his nose. "They're everywhere. All over the building," he said into his hands. "It's like a movie."

"Has there been an accident?"

"The janitor . . . Jack, you know . . . found a body when he came in this morning. A dead body."

"Where?" she asked.

"In the stacks."

"Was it . . . murder?"

"The police think he was killed after the library closed last night."

"Fiction or nonfiction?"

Mr. Upman took his hands from his face and considered Helma sternly. "I'm not making it up," he said indignantly.

"No, was the body in the fiction or nonfiction stacks?"

Mr. Upman shrugged. "I don't know. What difference does it make?" He paused as Helma waited. "Fiction stacks. In the Mo–Ne aisle, I think."

Miss Zukas was responsible for the nonfiction history and applied science sections.

"Who was it?"

Mr. Upman shrugged again. "They're not saying, but

from what I *have* heard, it might be a transient."

"Didn't you view the body?"

"Of course not."

Miss Zukas raised her eyebrows. Mr. Upman held the door for her and she entered the public service area ahead of him.

Despite being a large library for a city of thirty-five thousand, the Bellehaven Public Library was overcrowded and overused, with a book collection four times as large as the population and per capita circulation figures the envy of every librarian in the state. "With all this rain," Ruth had countered when Helma bragged about first quarter statistics, "what else is there for anyone with half a brain to do *except* read?"

The public service area was actually one large, open, L-shaped room divided by book stacks and tables. An addition four years ago had removed the children's collection to its own space downstairs, a decided improvement.

The staff, five librarians, seven clerks, and eight part-time pages, maintained a level of service that had once garnered a glowing sixty-second spot on the local TV station.

The library hadn't opened to the public yet but all the lights were on, cool fluorescence reaching between every narrow aisle of books, illuminating the corners and lowest shelves with pale light.

A knot of employees was gathered near the windows beside the philodendron plant, as far from the fiction shelves as possible. In its center, plump Mrs. Carmon, the morning circulation clerk, sobbed against Patty, one of the pages. The others huddled around her, patting shoulders and speaking in low voices. Off to the side, George Melville, the cataloger, and Roger Barnhard, the children's librarian, leaned together over the encyclopedia shelf, intently conversing. Eve, the librarian in charge of fiction, stood at the outer edge of the huddle, blond curls in disarray. She waved gaily at Helma, her eyes sparkling.

Official-looking men prowled the library building. Two policemen stood next to the card catalog, one writing in a notepad, the other whispering into a tape recorder. In the stacks, men in plain suits, but with that undefinable authoritative bearing, prodded among the books and squinted along the window ledges.

Murder. Murder in the library.

Helma allowed herself a dismayed shiver and then she firmly put the horror of it out of her mind. It was done. It was too late to alter what already existed. Only the facts could be dealt with now.

She sat at one of the two remaining oak library tables—the others had all been replaced by modern steel and wood-grained Formica—and removed her oxfords. Mr. Upman, dabbing at his forehead with his handkerchief, joined the library staff, who quickly enveloped him in their circle.

Helma slipped on the navy heels from her zippered case and tapped her feet lightly to settle into them. She smoothed down the lap of her skirt with her palms. Helma favored coordinated clothing; the blue of her skirt exactly mirrored the tail feathers of the Brazilian enameled bird pin on her burgundy sweater.

Helma touched her hair behind her ear to be sure that stubborn strand was in place. She'd worn the same becoming short and curled fashion for twenty years, since the day her mother had taken her to Dolly's Hair Salon back in Scoop River, Michigan, as a surprise sixteenth birthday present.

A yellow plastic tape stretched across the ends of the fiction stacks, separating the crime scene from the rest of the library. It read: POLICE LINE DO NOT CROSS.

Helma lifted the tape with one hand and smoothly ducked beneath it.

Four uniformed policemen and two men in suits stood talking beside the green-sheeted bulk on the floor. A redheaded policeman cleared his throat and caught the others' attention, nodding toward Miss Zukas, who had invaded their cordoned area.

"May I look?" she asked, stepping closer to the body.

It lay on the gray carpet under the green sheet, one dirty-knuckled hand peeping past a hem. Obviously a large body. The victim's feet protruded from beneath one end of the sheet: Rockports with untied laces.

There was a man, a murdered man beneath the green sheet. Helma paused, swallowing when there was nothing to swallow.

No, it was no longer a man. It was a body, just a body. Inanimate.

"The janitor will have a difficult time removing that stain," Helma observed, motioning to the deep red stain that curved beyond the sheet like a setting sun.

An ambulance attendant browsing through *Lolita*, looked up and said, "Probably have to replace the carpet."

"Ma'am," the red-haired policeman said, reaching for Helma's arm. "This is a police . . ."

"Excuse me," she told him and pulled back the green sheet.

The dead man lay on his stomach with his head turned to the side, toward Helma. His eyes were closed. Miss Zukas had never seen anyone dead who wasn't properly prepared in a casket and she'd read that the eyes of the dead remained open until someone else closed them. The victim looked to be about thirty, with brown hair and beard, matted like that of an uncombed dog or one of those musicians she sometimes caught sight of when she switched channels. He was dirty. His jeans and sweater had decayed to drabness and one elbow was worn through.

"I've seen this man before," she said to the policeman reaching for her arm, dropping the sheet so it billowed and settled back over the body.

They all turned their cool, detached policemen's eyes

toward her. She felt the intense stillness of their attention, their unblinking scrutiny.

"Would you mind telling us the circumstances?" one of the suited men asked.

Helma recognized Wayne Gallant, the Chief of Police. She tipped her head back to look into his face. Despite the gray at his temples, Chief Gallant's face was trapped between youth and middle age, smooth cheeks accented by laugh lines, clear eyes marred by dark circles.

"Yesterday afternoon he asked for one of the reference materials we keep behind the desk."

"Which reference material?" the chief asked.

Helma hadn't noticed them doing it, but as one, the policemen had all moved closer to her, surrounding her. Her nose twitched at the odor of after-shave and shoe polish.

Helma tried to remember. It had been a very busy day. Rainy days frequently drew the public into the library. It might have been a road atlas or an almanac.

"I'm sorry," she told him. "I can't recall right now, but I may later. I frequently do."

"Can you remember anything he said?"

"He requested a quarter to make a phone call."

"Did you give it to him?"

"I never give money to strangers," Helma assured the chief.

"Did you see him leave the library?" the other suited man asked, scribbling in a small, lined notebook.

Helma shook her head. "I was far too busy with my patrons to notice him leave." She waved her hand at the body, anonymous again under its discreet green covering. "If he was found in the library this morning, perhaps he never did leave."

"Is there any place he could have hidden?"

"There are probably several places. The library staff has too many workday responsibilities to patrol every nook and cranny."

"Do you remember anything else about him?" Chief Gallant asked. "How he walked, whether he was alone. Anything at all."

"No. As I said, it was a very busy day."

"We may want to ask you more questions later. Could you give Officer Sanderson here your name and telephone number?"

"Of course," Helma told him.

On the other side of the police line, she stopped and turned back. "One more thing," she said to Chief Gallant. "How did he die?"

"He was stabbed. It's probably long gone, but we're looking for the weapon now."

"Oh, Miss Zukas," Mrs. Carmon said as Helma joined the tense group of employees. She wiped her eyes with the cuff of her sweater. "How could you look?"

"It wasn't nearly as gruesome as one would expect," Helma told her.

"Did you recognize him?" Eve asked, pulling a damp yellow curl from her mouth and twisting it around her finger.

"He wasn't one of our regulars."

Mr. Upman agreed with Chief Gallant that yes, of course it was wisest to close the library for the day. The police took everyone's name and address and then told the staff to go home.

Helma stopped Mr. Upman beside the card catalog. "Shall we treat today like a Sunday as far as overdues are concerned?" she asked.

"Overdues?" he repeated. He waved his hand vaguely and tugged his tie further askew. "I don't know. I suppose if . . . Yes, do that. It's been a murder after all. Right here . . . I just . . ."

"Excuse me," a policeman interrupted. "There's a gray Buick in the parking lot blocking my cruiser."

"You were occupying my slot," Miss Zukas informed him. "I'll move it as soon as I change my shoes. It's the only parking place I'm entitled to while you policemen can legally park your cars anywhere you like in the entire city."

"Yes, ma'am. Thank you," he said.

"What are these, ma'am?" another policeman with dark eyebrows merging above his nose asked Helma, pointing to a stack of rods sitting on top of the card catalog.

"They're brass rods to hold bibliographic cards in the card catalog drawer," Helma explained. "They slide through holes in the bottom of the cards. We've been filing cards for new books."

"A tedious task," Mr. Upman added from behind Helma. "One that will go the way of the rumple seat when we computerize. Save us untold hours of staff time."

"That's 'rumble seat,' " Helma corrected. "And in my opinion, not that you've solicited the staff's opinion, the system we have now is perfectly adequate."

"Adequate is not . . ."

The stack of brass rods on top of the card catalog came unbalanced and clattered together under the policeman's inspection. Mr. Upman gasped and raised his hand to his chest.

The policeman pulled a white cloth from his pocket and picked up one of the rods. The brass knob was shiny but the length of the pointed shaft was stained dark, nearly black.

"I've found our weapon, Chief," he said loudly, triumphantly.

Chief Gallant quickly stepped between Helma and Mr. Upman and the policeman holding the rod.

"Thank you all very much for your cooperation," he said, even though Miss Zukas and Mr. Upman were the only staff members still in the library. He smiled a cool smile that didn't reach his eyes. "We'll call you if we have additional questions."

"The drawer rod itself is approximately the same

circumference as an arrow," Helma began. "With the proper force . . ."

"Thank you," the chief said again, motioning her and Mr. Upman toward the door through the workroom. "We'll be in contact."

Helma sat in the driver's seat of her car, both hands on the wheel. Her temples ached; there was an odd buzzing echo to everything she heard, like sound projected through water. She took two deep breaths, blinked hard, turned on the motor, and expertly backed her Buick out of the small library lot.

She drove through town, refusing to think about anything other than what she was seeing. She carefully stopped at each light, slowed past Emily Dickinson Elementary, determinedly noting the lush gardens already in bloom in Bellehaven despite the wet, gray spring. White and purple alyssum cascaded over rock walls and spilled down hillsides. Azaleas bloomed in brilliant reds and pinks against glossy greens. The big rhododendron by the park entrance was just peeking out blue, and Scotch broom misted pale yellow at its feet.

For a moment, sunshine emphasized the multiple muted colors on the Victorian house across from the Bayside Arms and then faded, leaving the house darkly drab.

In her apartment, Helma closed her drapes over the black plastic shades and turned on the sound track album from *The Sound of Music*. She changed into a blue T-shirt that said, "Book on into your local library," and her only pair of shorts: a pair of gym shorts she'd bought from a mail-order catalog five years ago.

Avoiding the damp spot on the carpet from her spilled plant, Helma concentrated on a half hour of exercises she normally did at 6:15 A.M. every Monday, Wednesday, and Friday, referring to a book titled, *Look Your Best at Any Age*, and which she credited for having kept her the same size as she'd been in high school. Today she did the Vigorous routine.

Even though it was the middle of the day, Helma decided to bathe after her exercises, and skip her bath that evening.

She plugged the tub's overflow drain with a wash-cloth and slid into the full tub, holding her breath against the water, which was as hot as she could stand it, watching her legs blush pink.

Murder.

Murders were uncommon enough in Bellehaven; maybe a rare killing in a back alley or in some uncontrolled domestic situation. But in the public library?

Occasionally at closing time, the staff discovered someone down on his luck trying to sleep undetected in the rest rooms or curled in the least-frequented areas of the library, like the corner by the political science section. Perhaps two transients had managed to hide in the library after closing and one had killed the other.

Helma considered the depths of passion and insanity one had to reach to take another's life, to forever steal away someone's future, to take away everything he or she had. It was unfathomable.

She placed the inflatable pillow, shaped like a sea-shell, behind her neck and leaned back. It was useless to spend any more time thinking about the murder, or murders in general. There simply wasn't enough available information for the former, and the latter was unplumbed alien territory.

After a cursory glance at her nails, she relaxed, letting her arms and hands go buoyant, clearing her mind.

Helma eschewed nail polish, although she manicured her fingernails and toenails on bath days and scrupulously washed and squeegeed her ears with Q-Tips on shower days. She kept an electric water-forced tooth and gum cleaner beside her bathroom sink. A warning came with it which read, "Do not use on personal body parts." Curious, Miss Zukas had, and found it quite pleasant, but usually she carefully tended her teeth with it and hadn't had a cavity in six years.

Helma toweled herself dry, noticing in her mirror how the warm water had heightened the freckles across her shoulders and arms and even the light smattering across her nose. In the midst of drying her back she was bowed by sudden, debilitating exhaustion. The towel was as heavy as lead. It was noon. She wasn't hungry. She didn't want to eat; she wanted to sleep. With her eyes already half-closed she dropped onto her bed, pulled up the afghan folded at the foot, and fell into a sound, dreamless sleep.

The telephone beside Helma's bed rang. She sat up, instantly wide-awake and alert, but let it ring twice more before she answered. She felt vaguely uncomfortable when people answered their phones after the first ring; as if it were rudely eager.

"Hello," she said. It was just past six o'clock.

"Oh, Helma. I just heard. Are you all right, dear? What a horrible thing to happen. Were you there? Did you see the body? Do they know who did it?"

Helma waited, knowing that sooner or later her mother would have to pause for breath.

"Eleanor Watt called to tell me and to ask if you'd already given me the news. Of course I told her that you were probably right in the thick of it and couldn't just drop everything to phone your mother with all the details. She heard it from Sarah, you know, the girl with that unfortunate voice who works in the deli? I've been so worried about you, dear. What a fright."

Her mother gasped for breath.

"I'm fine, Mother. I'm sure the police have the investigation under control."

"Did you see the body?" she asked again.

"Yes."

"Was it terrible, dear?" she asked hesitantly. "Was there a lot of . . . blood?"

"He'd been stabbed, so yes, there was an amount of blood. The police were already there when I arrived."

"Did you know him?"

"I think he was a transient. He wasn't a regular patron."

"Who'd kill anybody in a library? It's like that book by that British lady."

Helma held the telephone on her shoulder with her chin and glanced through her closet for another blouse. The blue one she'd pulled out earlier was creased across the sleeve.

"Mother," she said. "I don't know any more than you do. We'll just have to wait and see what the newspaper says."

"I suppose so." Her mother sighed, disappointed. "Do you think the library will be open tomorrow? I have two books due."

Helma's mother lived on the other side of Bellehaven in a retirement apartment complex with lots of light and chrome. A three-foot-tall sign on the lobby wall read, "OVER 55 AND READY TO JIVE!"

"Don't forget our lunch tomorrow," Helma's mother reminded her. "I can't wait to show you my campaign posters."

"I'm on the desk until one."

"That's not a problem for me. I'm hardly ever hungry. In fact, I might even forget to eat if people didn't remind me."

Helma and her mother had lunch together once a week and usually dinner on Sunday. Helma had convinced her mother to move from Michigan to Bellehaven three years ago, six months after Helma's father died and shortly after her mother discovered Helma's father had lied about the insurance.

Helma arranged a plate of scrambled eggs and asparagus on her table and opened her apartment door to retrieve the *Bellehaven Daily News*. More than once she'd requested that it be properly banded and lying on her doormat, but it rarely was. Tonight she found it between her door and Mrs. Whitney's in 3E, angled against the railing, the corner of the front page nearly torn off.

"MAN FOUND DEAD IN PUBLIC LIBRARY," the headline read, and in smaller print beneath it: "Police checking out foul play."

A photograph of the library accompanied the article. The picture had obviously been taken from the newspaper's files because roses bloomed outside the front entrance instead of azaleas and a few lingering tulips.

Aside from playing up the sensationalism of the crime, the news story told Helma nothing she didn't already know. Police were still uncertain how the victim or his murderer had gained admittance to the library after hours. There was no identification on the body, no known motive. Stab wounds to the chest. Helma noticed gratefully that the *Daily News* didn't mention that the murder weapon was a card catalog drawer rod.

She skimmed the other stories: a cocker spaniel nursed abandoned kittens; the city wanted to raise parking meter fees; the economy was definitely about to swing into an upturn.

Helma refolded the paper and went back to her dinner. The more things changed . . .

She bit into an asparagus tip just as her phone rang again. Helma never allowed phone calls to interrupt her meals, her bath, or Tom Brokaw. Her brother John in Iowa, who tended to call at dinner time, had sent her an answering machine last Christmas but luckily it was from Sears. Helma traded it back to Sears for a set of ironstone saucepans.

The phone quit in the midst of the sixth ring. It was probably Ruth. Helma wasn't up to discussing the more colorful side of the murder, and most certainly that's all Ruth would be interested in.

Helma opened her drapes and raised the plastic

shades. The sky was too clouded over for a colorful sunset. She stepped out onto her balcony and idly watched two sailboats, sails luffing in the calm gray evening, slowly circle a channel buoy. The air was moist against her cheek, portending rain. It was low tide and the bay was ringed with a glistening, rocky shoreline, dotted here and there by clam diggers and children investigating tide pools.

The phone rang again and this time she answered it.

"*Labas, labas,* Wilhelmina."

Helma had forgotten. "Aunt Em," she said contritely. "I'm sorry. There was a problem at the library."

"It's unlike you to forget to call, Wilhelmina. I was worried something was wrong."

Aunt Em was her father's older sister, the last of the six children still alive, and the only one—people back in Michigan used to say—with any common sense. It was Helma's habit to phone Aunt Em on Thursday evenings at five-thirty (eight-thirty in Scoop River, Michigan), just before Aunt Em had her cup of hot milk and went to bed.

"I'm fine," Helma assured her, "but something *was* wrong at the library today, Aunt Em. Someone died."

"Ah, people die too easy. Look how it is here. Did Brucie tell you Elsie Birzauski passed away last week? Stasys Mackavic and John Zamykas last month. Too soon, it seems like. Liddy Durbas is going, I hear."

Aunt Em was naming the old Lithuanians, children of the original early twentieth century immigrants, caught between two worlds all their lives and now in their seventies and eighties, like Aunt Em.

"*Myliu tave,*" Aunt Em said before she hung up. *I love you.*

Helma twisted the coiled telephone cord around her finger. "*Myliu tave,*" she replied with only a touch of self-consciousness.

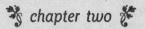

chapter two

THE LIBRARY
REOPENS

Friday morning, the sky was a high solid gray, without definition. The craggy peaks and slopes of the Canadian mountains jumbled the northern horizon. The islands to the west hunched one after the other, gray, like the sky, like the water.

As soon as she opened her curtains and took in the view, Helma firmly pulled down her plastic shades, just in case.

The broad street that led from Helma's apartment in the Bayside Arms to downtown Bellehaven followed the curve of the bay, twisting serenely along a bluff that overlooked the water. The street, locally referred to as "the boulevard," was a popular Sunday and sunset drive, with parklike pull-offs and walking trails that gently wound down to the rocky shore of Boardwalk City Park. As she drove to work, Helma glanced with pleasure at the gray water framed by the carefully tended roadside greens, all in soft, muted shades, nothing too bright or jarring.

Movement caught her eye and she glanced beneath her to see two men in a dinghy close to shore. She slowed her Buick, thinking what a striking photograph

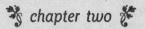

19

their silhouettes against the calm water would make. Why weren't there photographs like *this* in the *Daily News*, instead of aberrations of nature, like kittens suckling on dogs?

The men rowed toward a pink buoy marking a submerged crab pot. Crabbing in May, when most crabs were moulting and not very meaty, was a little out of season.

Maybe she'd research crabbing today, if the library was back to normal. As she braked at the first stoplight, just changing to yellow, ignoring the two sharp honks from the car behind her, she mapped out a course of action, beginning with shellfish and crustacean identification guides in the 595s, then on to the 639.54s where the books on fishing were shelved. She might even look up the crabbing laws—for her own satisfaction, of course.

Helma set her purse on her desk in the workroom and checked her lipstick in the mirror she kept in her desk drawer. Helma's desk sat between Patrice's and Eve's.

There were six librarians at the Bellehaven Public Library, including Mr. Upman the director: Eve, the fiction and music librarian; Helma, nonfiction history and applied sciences; Roger, the children's librarian; Patrice, the nonfiction social sciences and periodicals librarian; and George Melville, the cataloger. "Is that old Uppie's idea of egalitarianism?" Helma's friend Ruth had asked when she learned of the staff's sexual division. "In a field where ninety-five percent of the universe's librarians are women, he forges a staff that's fifty-fifty?"

During the remodeling only four years earlier, there hadn't been funds to expand the work area. The entire staff was jammed into the back room, a room that had grown to resemble a warehouse, with its stacks of books and files and desks. Mr. Upman's office and the tiny staff room were the only rooms with doors. The librarians' desks were arrayed on one side of the workroom, separated by four-foot-high bookshelves, and the cataloging staff and mendery tables were on the opposite side. Privacy was nonexistent.

The library didn't officially open until ten o'clock, and this morning the public area was uncomfortably quiet, heavy with an air of solemnity. Mrs. Carmon and two pages moved noiselessly as they put out newspapers and magazines. There was none of the loud conversation the younger pages especially liked to affect as if they were getting away with something forbidden.

Even the book trucks glided stealthily between the shelves as the staff reshelved books returned in the book drop overnight.

George Melville, the cataloger, stood by the card catalog stroking his beard. "Patty," he was saying in an uncharacteristically hushed voice as Helma passed. "Go downstairs and find me a drawer rod. I'm short one."

"Alone?" Patty asked, ending in a nervous titter.

"Yes, my dear. We're fresh out of escorts. And carry it pointy end down, please."

The ambulance attendant had been right: a six-foot section of carpet in the Mo–Ne fiction aisle had been removed and replaced by a new gray length, skillfully matched and seamed.

Helma toed the seam lines and found them tautly glued. One of the pages, holding an armload of books, stood at the end of the aisle watching her.

"Is there a problem, Curt?" she asked.

He swallowed, his Adam's apple disappearing behind his collar and reappearing again. "No. Not really. I just have to reshelve these books and . . ."

"You don't want to walk across the murder site," Helma finished.

He nodded, laughing in embarrassment.

"Give them to me. I'll do it," she said, stepping across the new carpet to take the books from him.

"Who do you think did it, Miss Zukas?" Curt asked.

"Obviously someone demented, but we can't let it interfere with our responsibilities to the public," she reminded him.

"Can't even tell somebody stumbled back there, can you?" George Melville asked when Helma emerged from the fiction section. "I heard they worked all night tidying up the place."

Mr. Upman had hired George Melville as cataloger three years ago. It was his first library job despite his being in his forties. "I suffered a mid-life career change," he liked to say dramatically, remarking he'd once been "in education." Eve didn't believe him; she was positive he'd been either a Shakespearean actor or a stand-up comic. Helma suspected he was a disgruntled minor bureaucrat. Patrice, on hearing Helma and Eve's discussion, announced that *she* believed George Melville and she wouldn't be surprised to hear he'd been dismissed from education on a morals charge.

At the circulation desk, Eve sat on a high stool with a stack of library magazines fanned in front of her, rapidly checking off her name on the routing slips. Helma doubted she'd opened a single one. A tiny Band-Aid was stuck to her chin. She grinned when she saw Helma glance at it. "A zit," she explained. "I wish I had skin like yours."

Eve was the newest and youngest librarian on the staff. Despite the fact that Eve didn't always take her position seriously, Helma found herself smiling whenever she unexpectedly came upon the curly-headed young woman. Once, Helma had stumbled over Eve sitting on the floor outside the downstairs children's room—where Helma suspected most of Eve's own reading material came from—playing at Barbie dolls with a young patron.

"It's kinda spooky around here, isn't it?" Eve said now. "Our leader has scheduled a meeting for eight-thirty: Librarians only. Maybe he's got the inside scoop on the murder. I was hoping we'd be closed another day, weren't you? Sort of like getting a snow day from school. I could have used it."

"Why?" Helma asked Eve. "What would you have done?"

"Looked for a new apartment."

"I thought you enjoyed living over a pizza shop."

"Oh yeah, it smells great." Eve frowned and bit the end of her pencil. "But it's my roommate. He . . . we don't get along so well anymore. Whose turn is it to clean the bathroom, who left dirty dishes in the sink, all that. You know."

Helma didn't. "I'll let you know if I hear of anything in my building," she told Eve.

"Thanks."

It was only 8:09. Time stood still. Helma found an empty book truck and pushed it toward the nonfiction shelves.

A year ago, Mr. Upman had taken over the process of weeding old books from the collection, explaining to the staff that as director, it was his "professional responsibility for adjustments to the collection."

Helma wouldn't have interfered if Mr. Upman actually *did* withdraw old books, but his method was haphazard, totally inefficient.

Helma's own system was simple and effective. She checked the due dates on the slip inside the book cover. If the book hadn't been checked out in three years and had no redeeming value that she could discern, out it went.

Every day or two, Helma advanced a little farther through the nonfiction stacks, withdrawing unread books. She was careful not to call attention to herself but she wasn't *sneaky* about it; not really. Naturally she'd stop if Mr. Upman ever caught on to what she was doing.

Fifteen minutes later the top shelf of her book truck was full of outdated and unread books from the 650s section. Helma brushed her hands together and wheeled the book truck to the end of the aisle. The air was jittery with the staff's nervousness.

Eve passed, heading for the workroom with her armful of library journals. "They shoulda left the body," she stage-whispered to Helma. "This place *feels* like a funeral parlor."

Near the reference collection, Mrs. Carmon and Lottie, the processing clerk, whispered together behind their hands, glancing toward the fiction stacks. Mr. Upman leaned against the A–Be shelf, chewing his lip and running his palm over his bare head, front to back. And yes, Helma had to admit, she herself was definitely walking with her weight balanced on the balls of her feet.

Suddenly Eve burst from the workroom into the public area and loudly confronted Mr. Upman.

"All right. Is this some kind of publicity stunt? Are we going to push mysteries by strewing the aisles with bodies, maybe hire little green men to walk around touting the pleasures of science fiction? What do you plan to do to advertise romance? This is a family library, I'd like to remind you."

Mr. Upman's mouth dropped open. "What, what . . ."

George Melville looked up from the card catalog and guffawed. Eve giggled.

Mr. Upman smiled uncertainly. "Oh, you're joking," he said. "A lame joke, Miss Oxnard."

Helma thought it was lame, too, but she gave an appreciative laugh. Eve's silliness had removed the murder one step further from their minds.

"You know," Mr. Upman said, speaking in a conversational tone again. "I heard about a library where they *did* separate their fiction collection into mysteries, romance, and science fiction."

"Don't forget westerns," George Melville added.

"That's an ancient concept," Eve said. "Nobody does that anymore."

"The modern theory being," George Melville said, "that in a mixed collection some poor fool who only reads westerns might accidentally pick up a 'real' book and broaden his horizons."

"Oh, mercy," Eve said, raising the back of her hand to her forehead.

"It was only an idea," Mr. Upman grumbled, stomping back to his office.

George Melville raised his eyebrows at Helma and Eve and shrugged.

Mr. Upman had become director four years earlier, after Mrs. Dorman, the previous director, had been confined to a nursing home.

Sometimes Helma suspected that Mr. Upman owed his library job to being a man. In a field dominated by women, a disproportionate number of library directors were men. "Library boards prefer male directors," she remembered Miss McKinney saying in library school, as if the female students might as well absorb that little fact right along with the Dewey decimal system and the Anglo-American cataloging rules.

"Meeting time, fellow professionals," George Melville said, pretending to hit a Chinese gong.

Helma sat between Eve and Roger Barnhard, the children's librarian. The five librarians and Mr. Upman circled the table in the staff lounge.

"More coffee, anyone?" Patrice asked, holding up the glass pot from the Mr. Coffee machine.

George Melville held out his cup. Before she poured, Patrice pulled a rumpled pink Kleenex from inside her sweater sleeve and dabbed up a drip on the lip of the pot.

George Melville hastily covered his cup with his hand. "No thanks," he said.

"Make up your mind," Patrice snapped.

Patrice had worked under three directors and was nearing retirement, although she'd flatly stated that she had no intention of retiring as long as she could perform her job, a subject that was already a matter of some speculation. Eve, who was somehow oblivious to Patrice's frequent barbs, felt sorry for her. "She's afraid of retiring. All she's got is that little old French poodle," Eve said sorrowfully.

Patrice set down the coffeepot and arranged herself in the chair across from Helma, using her cup and paper and pencils to define her space on the table. George Melville leaned an elbow perilously close to her border.

"Did you do it, Evie?" Roger hissed across Helma to Eve.

"Wouldn't you like to know," Eve said, wrinkling her nose at him.

"Beneath that Shirley Temple demeanor lurks the black heart of a murderer. I knew it all along."

"Shirley Temple," Eve sniffed. "*That's* demeaning."

"At least it happened up here," Roger said, rolling his eyes upward. "If it had happened down in the children's room, we wouldn't have been able to coax the kiddies back inside for weeks."

"Would've ruined your statistics, wouldn't it?" Eve teased, her hair brushing Helma's nose.

"Would you like me to move," Helma asked, "so you two can chat?"

"Of course not, Helma," Eve said, pouting. "Just make him stop picking on me."

"Children, children," George Melville said, putting his finger to his lips and nodding toward Mr. Upman, who sat tapping his pencil on his pad of yellow paper.

"Sorry, sir," Roger said, raising his hand in a mock salute.

Roger, who had the round, mischievous look of a Maurice Sendak illustration, wasn't as tall as many of the children who visited his department. More than once Helma had gone to the children's room and found Roger's staff running the department while Roger sat in his office reading financial magazines. She'd never met his wife but Helma had seen them walking on the street with their four children like steps—with Roger occupying the third step down, after his wife and a son.

Mr. Upman cleared his throat, bringing the meeting to order. "As you all know, we've been the scene of an alarming tragedy," he said.

"Oh really?" Roger mumbled so low only Helma heard.

"We can expect the investigation to disrupt our lives for days to come," Mr. Upman continued. "I've given the police permission to investigate wherever and whenever they wish, and it's imperative that each of us cooperate to the fullest."

"I'm sure I speak for all of us when I say you can count on our cooperation, Mr. Upman," Patrice said, glancing around the table, her eyes resting on each of them.

"My cataloging department's an open book," George Melville deadpanned.

Roger slapped the table and Eve giggled. Patrice's back stiffened. Her eyes, which habitually beamed on the men and belittled the women, narrowed on George.

"We'll all cooperate, of course," Helma interrupted. "Are there any developments in the investigation?"

Mr. Upman shook his head, his eyes large behind his thick glasses. "There's no new information as far as I know."

Patrice shuddered and tapped her glasses against her substantial chest. "When we allow people like that into our library, we have to expect murder and mayhem."

"We can't very well screen our patrons at the door," George said.

"That's right," Mr. Upman agreed. "Whether we like it or not, we are a public institution."

"I went swimming in a public pool in Ohio once where they inspected our feet before they allowed us into the water," Eve said. "That was a public institution."

Roger looked at Eve speculatively. George scratched his ear.

"And your point is?" Patrice asked, her nostrils flaring.

Eve shrugged and twisted a curl. "I don't know," she said in a small voice.

Mr. Upman cleared his throat and teeter-tottered his pencil between his fingers. "Just remember: in a time of crisis like this, we must never forget our patron."

"Not that our patron would ever let us," George Melville muttered.

"And now we must move on to other business," Mr. Upman continued. "Time doesn't stand still even in the face of tragedy. Plans for computerizing our card catalog continue. I'm nearing a decision on the vendor, so you'll be seeing a few vendors' representatives returning to the library. Please be courteous to them, despite whatever feelings you have about the project."

"Replacing the card catalog is an unnecessary financial burden," Patrice said. "It's served us well all these years."

"Thank you, Patrice," George Melville said, inclining his head graciously. "I do my best."

Patrice reared back and snapped her mouth closed, momentarily at a loss.

"If we'd been computerized, there wouldn't have been any drawer rods handy for the murderer to use," Roger pointed out.

"Oh, *there's* a plus," George Melville said.

"The murderer could have electrocuted him," Eve offered.

Helma raised her hand slightly to catch Mr. Upman's attention. "My concern is that the staff hasn't been involved with this project. If you were to choose a representative to voice the staff's interests, we might be more enthusiastic. I have several questions: we *are* discussing MARC format, aren't we? And keyword searching?"

Mr. Upman doodled boxes and pyramids on his yellow pad. "Of course you'll all be involved later. But at the present time, administrative decisions are in order, not committees."

Helma closed her mouth and doodled bull's-eyes on her own pad of paper.

When the meeting broke up, Patrice tapped Helma's arm as she pushed in her chair. "Can't you control that child?" she asked.

"I beg your pardon?"

"Eve." Patrice's mouth tightened. "Can't you say a few words to make her realize the seriousness of the situation? Everything's a game to her. I doubt she has the qualifications to stay very long in the field."

"Are we speaking of corn or hay fields?" George Melville asked from behind Patrice. "And which one are you more familiar with?"

Patrice raised her hand to her throat. Her eyes flashed. "I wasn't speaking to you. You're hardly qualified to distinguish seriousness from frivolity." And she wheeled and left the staff room.

"That woman walks like she has a corncob . . ." He stopped and shrugged at Helma. "The old biddy," he said and strode off in the same direction as Patrice, leaving Helma alone with Mr. Upman.

Mr. Upman tore the top sheet of paper from his yellow pad and crumpled it between his hands. "These meetings . . ." he said to Helma. "They never go quite like I plan. The staff . . ."

"Excuse me, don't forget I'm a member of the staff," Helma interrupted and left Mr. Upman crumpling his paper into an ever smaller wad.

❧ chapter three ❧

CHIEF GALLANT AND RUTH VISIT THE LIBRARY

"This may not boost our circulation but it certainly increases the traffic flow," Eve said to Miss Zukas when Curt unlocked the double glass doors to the public at ten o'clock and a long line of patrons filed into the library, their heads swiveling as they searched for evidence of murder.

"Mysteries should be a good mover today," Helma replied.

"You bet," Eve said and gave Helma a thumbs-up sign. "Since I'm the fiction librarian, do you think I should give tours? I could point out a few good books before we reach the fatal aisle."

"I'm not sure Mr. Upman would approve," Helma said.

"I'm joking," Eve assured Helma. "Honest."

At 10:59 Helma relieved Patrice at the reference desk. The reference desk was the "front line" of library service, where patrons stopped to ask questions that ranged from "Where's the pencil sharpener?" to "What does the half-moon on the outhouse door mean?"—a question they'd yet to answer adequately.

"Has it been a busy morning?" Helma asked.

Patrice removed her glasses and let them hang by their gold chain against her bosom. "There have been several very difficult questions," Patrice told Helma. "It was fortunate I was on the desk. I'll be in the workroom if you have any problems and require my help."

"I'll keep that in mind," Helma said.

She watched Patrice's stiff, almost mincing steps as she returned to the workroom, wondering what the rest of George Melville's reference to Patrice's walk and the corncob would have been.

"I'm from Destiny Computer Systems," the man in front of Helma announced before she could offer her assistance, "and I'm here to see Mr. Upman."

He was young and carefully barbered and regarded Helma without interest. His light gray suit was uncreased and he tapped manicured fingers against the hard side of his black briefcase.

One of the computer vendors. Helma had seen him several times over the past year wooing Mr. Upman. Obviously he was one of the finalists for the computerized catalog system. She didn't recall his being so impatient. Perhaps that's what being close to winning did.

"Yes?" she asked.

"Call him and tell him I'm here," he ordered, then hastily added, "please."

Helma frequently did just that when she was on the reference desk, but she did it as a courtesy, not because she was ordered to.

"I'm a professional librarian with more pressing duties," she politely informed the man from Destiny Computer Systems. "You may ask a staff member at the circulation counter to help you."

He studied her coldly for a second too long and turned away.

The security alarm beeped and Helma heard Mrs. Carmon cheerfully tell a middle-aged man, "Whoops! I think you forgot to check out a book," giving him

every benefit of the doubt. Most patrons were aware of
the square security stickers inside each book that set off
the alarm if the book wasn't checked out and desensi-
tized. But someone always tried it anyway.

"Lady?"

Helma looked across the desk into the dark eyes of a
boy about nine. He wiped his nose on the frayed cuff
of his jacket.

"You may call me Miss or Ma'am," she said in her
silver-dime voice. "And the children's room is downstairs."

"I know that, Miss. I wanna see where they found
the dead guy."

"Why aren't you in school?"

"My teacher got sick," the boy said, glancing away.
"They couldn't find a substitute so . . . so they sent us
all home."

"Where's your mother?"

The boy waved vaguely. "She doesn't come to
libraries."

"I see. Do you?"

The boy shrugged. "Once, with my class."

Helma considered the boy. The hardest part was
coaxing them *into* the library. Once that was accomplished they were usually hooked. She leaned forward.
"Would you like a private tour of the crime scene?"

His eyes widened and a dimple appeared in one
cheek. "Wow! Way cool!"

"I suspect that's an affirmative reply. Excuse me and
I'll make the arrangements."

Helma buzzed Eve's desk. "There's a young man at
the reference desk who's requested your crime tour,"
she said. "He might also be enticed into choosing a
mystery from downstairs."

"Cool!" Eve said.

Helma found the full name of the emir of Kuwait,
gave directions to the rest rooms, searched out bio-

graphical information on the Italian sculptor Benvenuto Cellini, and had just found a misfiled topographical map of Mt. Baker when Mr. Upman leaned over her with his mouth uncomfortably close to her ear and said, "Excuse me, Miss Zukas. Chief Gallant will be here in about ten minutes to ask you a few more questions. I'll relieve you of your desk duties when he arrives."

"I've already told him everything I know," Helma said, leaning away from Mr. Upman's shiny face. Then seeing his frown, she sighed. "I suppose the police find it necessary to keep reviewing the details until something new comes to light."

Mr. Upman patted her shoulder and said soothingly, "Now, don't be concerned about the questions, Miss Zukas. I'm sure they'll be simple to answer if you just tell the truth."

"Honestly answering a policeman's questions has never caused me concern, Mr. Upman, I assure you," she said and turned to a young woman with a baby in a snuggle bag against her chest.

"How may I help you?" Helma asked, leaning toward the young woman so that, behind her, Mr. Upman was dismissed.

"I have the telephone number of a man who wanted to buy my car," the woman said, shifting her baby, "but I lost his name and the telephone operator won't give it to me. Can you help me?"

"Was it a Bellehaven number?"

The woman nodded.

"You need to look in the reverse phone listings of the city directory," Helma told her. "I'll get it for you."

Questions that could be answered by the city directory were some of the questions most commonly asked by patrons. Who's my next door neighbor? Where does he work? Is the man I met last night married? Does he own his house? All were questions it took the least effort for the librarians to answer and for which library patrons were the most effusively grateful. Helma couldn't figure it out.

Helma wheeled her desk chair around to face the shelves behind her. As she touched the spine of the *Polk's City Directory*, she remembered.

The murdered man had asked to see this very directory. She'd have new information to give Chief Gallant after all.

"We request you use it here at the reference desk," Helma told the young woman. If the directory was let out of the librarians' sight, it was frequently returned with missing pages, even though Mr. Upman insisted there be pencils and scratch paper scattered throughout the library.

A scrap of yellow paper fluttered from the directory as she handed it to the woman. Helma picked it up and set it on her desk while she demonstrated how to use the reverse telephone number section.

The yellow paper, raggedly torn on two edges, appeared to have been ripped from a notice, or, Helma frowned, from the end pages of a book. On it were the letters SQ VILKE HCR, followed by two dates: Mar. 10 and April 7, then the phrase, "1649 or 1469." It made no sense.

Patrons frequently used shreds of napkins, grocery store receipts, envelopes, or hairpins as bookmarks. Once a book with a crisply fried piece of bacon between its pages had been shoved down the book slot.

Helma was already asking, "How may I help you?" when she recognized Chief Gallant.

"Miss Zukas," he acknowledged, nodding.

"Chief Gallant."

He held his hat in front of him. Chief Gallant was one of the few men in Bellehaven who wore a hat to top off his suit. He smiled slightly at Helma, his eyes crinkling and forming lines that aged his face, but not unhandsomely. Chief Gallant's body had the air of being too large for his suit, as if touching his elbows together might split the back of his jacket. Helma remembered reading he'd been a football star in college, or maybe it was basketball. Now he looked as though he exercised just enough to keep the excess weight at bay.

"I'd like to ask you a few questions, if I may?"

"Of course," she said, and waited.

"Could we go somewhere more private?"

"Please. Use my office. It's empty."

It was Mr. Upman, holding out his hand to Chief Gallant.

"That will be fine," Chief Gallant said, shaking Mr. Upman's hand. "Thank you."

Helma slipped the yellow scrap of paper into her skirt pocket and led Chief Gallant toward the workroom, hearing Mr. Upman's cheery voice behind her, asking brightly, "Now what can I do to help *you*?"

Mr. Upman's office was scrupulously tidy. "The Sanctuary," Eve called it.

Helma sat down behind Mr. Upman's desk. Chief Gallant looked disconcerted for a moment, and then shut the office door and lowered himself into one of the upholstered chairs facing the desk. He balanced his hat on his crossed knee.

"What would you like to ask me?" Helma asked, folding her hands on Mr. Upman's desk blotter.

"I have a record of everyone's statements here," Chief Gallant said. He removed a notebook from his breast pocket, flipped a few pages, and paused to read, one finger tracing along the page. Then he asked, "You thought you recognized the murder victim as having asked a library question?"

"No."

Chief Gallant frowned at his notebook. "That's what I have."

"I said I *did* recognize the man, not that I *thought* I recognized him."

"You're certain?"

Miss Zukas sat straighter. "Of course."

Chief Gallant touched his pencil to his tongue. He smiled, the left corner of his mouth higher than the right. "Why don't you tell me everything you remember?"

"It was about four-thirty. I was on duty at the reference desk and I looked up and there he was . . ."

"Describe him, if you would."

"About six feet, thin, brown hair, brown untrimmed beard, thirty to thirty-five. Unkempt appearance." Helma delicately wrinkled her nose. "He had an odor of cigarettes and I doubt if he'd been near a bath in some time."

"Did he seem nervous or agitated?"

Helma considered the question, then tapped her index finger on the desk. "No, not nervous, but while he was speaking to me, his right eye twitched. That might indicate nervousness, don't you think?"

"Possibly." Chief Gallant wrote rapidly in his notebook. "You said you weren't certain about the library question he'd asked you?"

"I said that, yes, but I just remembered. He asked to see the city directory. It's one of our most popular reference books. You're familiar with it, of course?"

The chief nodded. "We have a copy in the office. Did you notice what he was looking up?"

"I respect my patrons' privacy, Chief Gallant."

"I'm sure you do, Miss Zukas. Did he say anything else to you, ask for any other information besides the city directory? Did you see him talk to anyone else?"

Helma shook her head. "He spent perhaps ten minutes looking through the directory. He mumbled a few times under his breath, but it was nothing I could make out. Then he handed the directory back to me and that's when he asked for a quarter for the pay phone. That's the last I saw of him—until yesterday morning, of course."

The chief leaned forward and peered across the desk into Helma's face. His blue eyes were uncomfortably piercing. "Can you remember anything he mumbled while he was looking through the directory, anything at all, even if it didn't make any sense to you?"

Helma thought of the brown-haired, disheveled man. She had tried to stay as oblivious of him as possible, with his odor and all. She frowned at the framed saying that hung on the wall over the chief's head. "Today is the first day of the rest of your life," it read.

Chief Gallant scratched his ear with the eraser end of his pencil. His big body was loose, relaxed, as if he had all the time in the world to wait until Helma remembered some trivial fact. Anything. Helma was extremely busy. She had work to do. April's circulation and reference statistics still weren't tallied.

"I think," she said slowly, "I'm not positive, mind you, but he might have said something like, 'Four, not nine.' "

The chief wrote it quickly in his notebook, smiling at her as if she'd been a very clever child.

"Now, one last question. Did you notice anyone else take an interest in this man? Are you sure you didn't catch a glimpse of him again after he left the reference desk?"

"I'm much too busy to notice the interactions between patrons in the library. The Bellehaven Public Library is the busiest library, per capita, in the state. We're underfunded, short-staffed, threatened by budget cuts. We've outgrown our facilities, even though an addition was built four years ago. Do you think the overburdened public would pass another bond issue for a second addition, or for a new building, which is what we really need?"

Chief Gallant snapped his notebook closed and held up his hand. "I know, I know. Every city department faces the same problems." He took his hat from his knee and stood. "We all do the best we can. You people in the library deserve recognition for the outstanding job you do; there's no doubt about that."

"Thank you," Miss Zukas said modestly. "Now that I've answered your questions as best I can, Chief Gallant, don't you feel it would be fair to disclose what you've discovered regarding this murder?"

"There are no secrets to divulge, I'm afraid," the chief said. "We have an unidentified male, stab wounds to the chest. No suspect. No motive. As far as we know, he wasn't seen around town before Wednesday. We do have a report of a transient of another description in the vicinity of the library the night of the murder."

"But how did they get inside?"

"We found footprints that matched the prints of the victim's shoe soles on a toilet seat in the men's room."

"So he *did* stay in the library after it closed. What about the murderer?"

Chief Gallant absently lifted his hat to his head, then seeing Helma's glance, dropped his arm and tapped his hat against his pant leg. "We suspect the victim let him in," he said.

"Why would you think that?" Helma asked.

The chief placed his hand on the doorknob. "The hall floor near the Webber Street exit had recently been waxed. A number of his footprints were evident near the door."

"As if he'd been waiting for someone," Helma finished. "Were there fingerprints?"

"None by the door that we could find. What we found upstairs was pretty inconclusive."

"It seems that if the murder had been premeditated, the weapon would have been something other than a card catalog drawer rod, something brought from *outside* the library."

"That's possible." Chief Gallant removed a card from his pocket and handed it to Helma. "I'll be here a while longer to talk to some of the other staff members. If you think of anything else at all, no matter how inconsequential it seems, please contact me."

Helma took the card, glancing at both his office and

home phone numbers printed on it. "I will, although I'm confident I've told you all I remember."

"You never know when a stray thought may pop into your head," he said.

She blanched at the idea of stray thoughts popping about, and left Chief Gallant to quiz his next subject.

Helma's throat was dry, almost parched. She didn't drink from drinking fountains so she stopped by the staff lounge for a glass of water.

Patrice and Mrs. Carmon stood together by the coffeepot.

"Well, what kind of dog is causing all the trouble?" George Melville, who sat at the table with a powdered sugar donut, looked up and asked Patrice.

"A spaniel, I think," Patrice answered warily. "That's right, an English springer spaniel. Binky's terrified of him."

"Then the reason's obvious. The French and the English have never got along."

Patrice gave a tiny, uncertain laugh.

As she rinsed her glass, Helma wondered if what Eve said was true, that all Patrice had in the world was Binky, her French poodle.

Without really meaning to listen, Helma had overheard talk that there was a husband somewhere in Patrice's distant past. A postal employee, the talk said, who'd shadowed Patrice faithfully for years before he began drinking and became shadowier and quieter and finally drifted out of Patrice's life altogether. Somebody made the unkind comment that it was three months before Patrice noticed he was gone.

Mr. Upman slapped closed a copy of *Art & Antiques* magazine when he saw Helma. He discouraged the staff from reading while they tended the reference desk. "Patrons feel uncomfortable interrupting you to ask a question," he'd said.

"That artist friend of yours was here to see you," he

told Helma. "She said she'd be back in ten or fifteen minutes."

"Are you referring to Ruth Winthrop?" Helma asked, knowing he was.

"Who else?" he asked stiffly.

After Helma had seen Mr. Upman jogging in his surprisingly healthy body, she had told her friend Ruth, who had gone quiet and uncharacteristically thoughtful. Helma suspected that Ruth had stalked Mr. Upman into his or her bed, then moved on once her curiosity was satisfied. All Ruth had finally said was, "What a waste to have the brain of a Marx Brothers librarian connected to the body of an Olympic marathoner."

By the sudden hushed silence, Helma knew before she saw her that Ruth had entered the library. Hushes and glances usually preceded and followed Ruth's appearances.

Ruth was a half inch over six feet tall and extended her height by favoring high-heeled boots and multicolored turbans or piling her bushy hair on top of her head. Seeing Ruth's proportions was a jolt in itself without considering her garishly mismatched outfits, usually sewn for herself because she couldn't find clothes to fit her long body.

Ruth preferred dramatic colors: bright purples and deep reds and oranges, sometimes wearing them all at once. She made up her piercing eyes with black kohl, à la Colette, and wore earrings the size of Helma's fists.

Today Ruth wore an outfit of three different shades of red, not one of them a shade Helma would wear. It was a dress of sorts, but the seams and hemlines were not in their accustomed places.

Ruth dropped onto the edge of the reference desk with a grunt and said, "Tell me the truth. Did you kill the bum?" in such a sotto voice that Helma got goose bumps from the stares of every patron within hearing range.

Ruth's face was as overproportioned as her body: her wide mouth and broad, high cheekbones, her large nose that incongruously turned up at the end, her too-far-apart eyes.

"Hello, Ruth," Helma whispered.

"Helm," Ruth responded at a conversational level.

"Helma," she corrected, as she always did.

"Helma," Ruth repeated, pronouncing it "Hell-mah" as she always did. "I thought I'd find you womaning the Reverence desk."

"Reference," Helma amended, even as she noted the satisfied glint in Ruth's eye. She couldn't help it; it was impossible to ignore Ruth's habit of trivializing serious matters.

A man in workman's clothes approached the desk. Ruth winked at him and swung her leg back and forth. The man veered away toward the shelves of telephone books.

"Did I scare him away?" Ruth whispered.

"You do look slightly . . . intimidating," Helma told her.

Ruth pulled the corners of her mouth down in a petulant frown.

Ruth and Helma were the same age; they'd known each other since they were ten, back in Scoop River, Michigan, when they'd been placed together at the end of every alphabetical list: Winthrop, Zukas. As children, they'd sometimes fantasized they'd been switched at birth. Ruth had towered over her own father, fitting more easily into Helma's oversize, overexuberant family, where Helma was the smallest and the least noticeable, not even as tall as Ruth's father.

Ruth had followed a lover from Michigan to Santa Fe to Seattle eight years earlier and had eventually ended up—minus the rock musician-lover—in Bellehaven's slowly growing arts community. Sometimes when Helma looked at Ruth, beneath the towering self-confidence she saw a hunched-over eleven-year-old girl, crying bitterly behind the school because she'd been taunted too often about her height and casual personal habits.

"What's the skinny?" Ruth asked, leaning closer across the desk. "Any clues from the gestapo?"

The pungency of Ruth's perfume settled over the reference desk, along with the oily smell of paint that inevitably accompanied Ruth.

"No clues," Helma told her. "I think this crime may turn out to be one of those unsolved mysteries."

"Don't underestimate our local crime solvers," Ruth said, shaking her finger at Helma, her bracelets clinking. "But in the library; who'd commit murder in the sanctity of the library?"

Ruth lived hand to mouth: high when her paintings were selling; below poverty when they weren't, never saving for the lean times. She drank too much, had too many affairs, ate like a lumberjack, was never on time—just as likely to be too early as too late. When Ruth's painting was going well, she might disappear for days, locking herself in her house and not answering her telephone. When she couldn't paint, she roamed Bellehaven, hollow-eyed and hyperactive, stirring up attention and, frequently, trouble.

Helma was bewildered as to how and why she and Ruth were still friends. Being with Ruth for more than an hour left her exhausted and ready for a nap.

"I don't suppose there's any proper place for a murder, is there?" Helma asked.

Helma had been fielding questions from two or three patrons at a time before Ruth entered the library. Now, suddenly, no one approached the reference desk. Ruth sprawled across it, leaning on one elbow.

"I think the guy had overdue books and Upman lured him to his death. What do you want to bet he stabbed him with the pointy end of his pencil?"

Ruth made thrusting movements with her fist, stabbing at the air between Helma and herself. Helma cleared her throat meaningfully, but Ruth paid no attention.

"Actually," Helma told her. "The murder weapon was a rod from a card catalog drawer."

"No kidding? Is that an efficient use of local resources, or what? How'd the guy get in?"

"He stood on a commode in the men's room and no one saw him at closing."

Ruth waved her hand in disgust. "That's one of the oldest tricks on the books. Don't you ever check the toilet stalls?"

"I never check the men's room at all."

Ruth nodded and with one finger, spun the circular pencil holder. "I suppose not, but you should, you know. It gives you a whole new perspective on bodily functions."

Helma glanced down at her desk top. The card with Chief Gallant's phone number sat in front of her. She couldn't imagine calling his home, whether she had new information or not. Ruth followed her gaze.

"You've got his home phone number. It's unlisted, you know. There are a lot of women who'd consider murder most foul for that little scrap of information."

"Why?"

Ruth laughed her deep hiccupy laugh. A gray-haired woman at the newspaper rack looked up and shook her head.

"Because the chief is prime material, you goose. Very aloof since his divorce. With the man/woman ratio in this town, he created quite a stir when his number came up."

"Are you interested in him?" Helma asked.

Ruth winked. "Let's just say I'm not interested in him anymore."

Helma changed the subject. "How's the new painting progressing?"

The teasing light in Ruth's eyes switched to dark shade. She hunched her shoulders and rubbed her arms as if she were chilled.

"Ugh. There's something wrong with it but I can't figure out what. I sat in front of it for three hours last night and nothing made any sense. I've gotta get somebody else to look at it."

Helma didn't offer and she knew Ruth didn't expect her to. Ruth's paintings left Helma uneasy and troubled. She had tried to explain to Ruth how she felt. How art should be controlled, showing the artist's skill at rendering reality, not so . . . raw. Ruth hadn't seen any farther into Helma's explanation than the fact that her art just wasn't Helma's "cup of tea."

"You OK?" Ruth asked.

"I'm sorry. I was thinking," Helma told her.

"Solving the murder?"

"I'll leave that to the police."

"Our skilled boys will have it wrapped up in no time." Ruth pulled up her sleeve to glance at her over-size man's watch. "Gotta go. I'm meeting a neophyte artist who's come to worship at my feet. Lunch at Perdighi's. I'll probably have to pay. Want to come?"

Helma shook her head. "I'm having lunch with my mother."

Ruth stood and shook her body until her clothes hung almost straight. "I suppose she's eager to hear the goriest details?"

"Rumors *are* making the rounds. She naturally wants to know the facts."

"Of course. 'Just the facts, ma'am.' See ya."

Ruth took two long strides away from the reference desk and turned around. "Have you thought any more about . . . you know . . . forgiving me my trespasses?"

Helma shook her head. Ruth was barred from checking out library books because she owed $86.47 in overdue fines and Helma refused to use her influence to get the fine dropped from Ruth's record.

Ruth wrinkled her nose at Helma. "Just think of the government's efficiency rate if they had a few thousand of you, Helm," she said, and stalked out of the building.

Helma removed Chief Gallant's card from the top of the desk and slipped it into her pocket. As she did, she touched the yellow scrap of paper that had fallen from the Bellehaven city directory. She pulled it out and smoothed it flat on the reference desk.

It was just gibberish some patron had distractedly scribbled while looking at the directory. With a pencil, Helma doodled on the yellow paper, tracing around "SQ VILKE HCR," drawing a box around "Mar. 10" and "April 7," and sketching flowers in the corners.

Then, guiltily, she jerked away her pencil. She was defacing personal property. She recopied the letters and numbers onto a clean sheet of notepaper as exactly as she could, even the odd way the writer had formed his or her 6s and 7s. The owner might come back to reclaim it. It could be some kind of a word game.

"Excuse me."

A middle-aged man in a blue suit stood in front of Helma. She'd been dealing with the public long enough to recognize someone who wasn't from Bellehaven, or at least wasn't used to the relaxed courtesy of the public library.

"How may I help you?" Helma asked.

He clicked a Mont Blanc pen, holding it poised over a blank page in a leather-bound notebook. "I'm looking for a good private college for my son. Can you show me how to locate some comparative data?"

"You want the Peterson Guides," Helma told him. "They're on the shelf next to the microfiche reader."

"Over there?" the man asked, pointing toward the listening booths.

Helma Zukas rarely pointed, and never inside a building. "No," she said. "Behind you and slightly to your left."

As he turned in the opposite direction, his notebook slipped from his hands and fell onto the desk.

"How clumsy. I apologize," he said, leaning forward and picking it up.

Helma's pad of paper caught in his notebook and he lifted them both from the desk top.

"Excuse me," Helma said. "But you've accidentally picked up my notepad."

"I'm sorry," he said, loosening the pad and setting it precisely where it had been on the desk.

"That's quite all right," Miss Zukas assured him.

"Now I see the shelf you're talking about. I appreciate your help."

Another patron asked for a copy of an old newspaper. A woman with a bandage around her arm asked where the books on venomous snakes were shelved. An elderly gentleman with a cane complained that the day's *Wall Street Journal* hadn't listed his stock. Helma gave him the phone number of two local brokerage firms.

At one o'clock, Eve arrived to relieve her.

"Been busy?" Eve asked.

"The usual."

"You know what I've been doing?"

"No, I don't," Helma said.

Eve shook her head so her yellow curls bounced. "I've been checking the books on the Me–No aisle for blood."

"Did you find any?"

"Not even a suspicious rust-colored spot. I think our leader was disappointed. It was his idea; he didn't want any of our patrons to innocently pluck a bloodspattered book off the shelf."

Helma straightened the desk top for Eve, replacing the pencil in the holder, aligning the notepad and the telephone.

"George told me there's an apartment open in his building," Eve said. "Do you think it would be too

weird to live in the same building as a guy you work
with?"

The yellow slip of paper was gone. Helma checked
the floor and under the desk pad, behind the telephone.

"Lose something?" Eve asked.

"One of the patrons left a yellow slip of paper in the
city directory," Helma told her, frowning. "It was right
here on top of the desk. I thought he or she might come
back for it."

Helma shook out the phone book and then tore off
the first page of the notepad, where she'd copied the
letters and numbers.

"I do have a copy if anyone comes looking for it,"
Helma told Eve.

The man who'd asked about the college guides was
gone. He certainly hadn't spent much time at his task.
It was odd he'd been so clumsy, dropping his notebook
on the desk like that. He hadn't seemed the awkward
type. He might have accidentally picked up the yellow
paper along with his notebook.

It was fortunate, she thought, slipping her hand into
her pocket and fingering the folded notepaper resting
against Chief Gallant's card, that she'd made a copy of
the yellow piece of paper in case its owner returned.

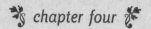

chapter four

THE INCIDENT IN SAUL'S DELI

"**D**o you like this color?" Helma's mother asked, touching the blue flowered scarf at her neck.

"It goes well with your eyes," Helma said as she dipped her tea bag twice and spooned it out, wrapping the string around the bowl of the spoon so the last of the amber liquid squeezed into her cup.

Helma's mother smoothed her silver blond hair with her palm and tipped her head, smiling gently at her reflection in the window. Helma noticed her mother was gaining weight again. The buttons of her blouse pulled dangerously taut across the front.

"You don't think it's too bright?"

"I think it's fine, Mother."

"Well, I want to be sure."

Helma's mother sliced the crusts from her avocado and cream cheese sandwich and then cut each half sandwich in half again.

"This is way too much for me to eat," she said. "They give you such big servings." She folded the crusts inside a napkin and set them at the edge of the table like a gift package.

Saul's Deli was crowded. Fortunately, Helma had noticed two women getting up from the window table and had stood beside it while the waitress cleared and wiped it off. Three women and a well-dressed couple still waited by the door.

Helma ate a plain roast beef sandwich on white bread, without mustard or mayonnaise, just a little butter. She waited for her mother to mention the murder.

Helma's mother's name was Lillian, named because her own mother had been enamored of the tinselly glitter of Hollywood, in particular Lillian Gish. Lillian kept a gossamer photo of Lillian Gish over the sofa in her retirement apartment. "I'm her namesake," Lillian liked to say with a mysterious smile when she was asked about the photo. For a while when Helma was a child, her mother had worn her hair like old publicity shots of Lillian Gish in *Broken Blossoms*.

"Are you going to eat your dill?" Lillian asked.

"No. Would you like it?"

"Rather than let it go to waste."

Helma forked the dill pickle and transferred it to her mother's plate. Lillian held out her bowl of fruit. Only some miniature species of Concord grapes were left.

"Would you like a grape?"

"I don't eat purple food," Helma reminded her.

"Of course, dear. I forgot."

Using her fork and knife, Lillian tidily cut the dill pickle into half-inch disks. Then she leaned across the table and said in a husky voice, "Now, dear. I want you to tell me about the murder—the *real* story, not the silly blather that's in the *Daily News*."

Helma sighed. "There is no *real* story, Mother. The police are as mystified as everyone else. The victim was unknown. He concealed himself in the library until after it closed and was stabbed, just as the paper reported. Chief Gallant said there was no sign of forced entry; the victim might have let his murderer in the library himself."

"Chief Gallant? You talked to Chief Gallant?"

"He *is* the Chief of Police."

Lillian waved her fork with a slice of pickle on the end and sadly shook her head. "That poor, poor man. The way his wife just up and left him like that. I heard she had a moving van at the house, bold as brass, while he was away at his office. She even took his bureau, can you imagine? Left all his clothes and a sleeping bag piled in the middle of the bedroom floor. Such a tragedy and him such a good, kind man. You can tell just by looking at him. Did it seem to you that he's getting over his heartbreak?"

"We didn't discuss his personal life."

Lillian glanced vacantly over Helma's head and bit her lower lip, a habit Helma recognized. Her mother was thinking about something she'd like to say but knew she'd better not.

"Well, no matter; it's a tragedy. Any woman would be crazy not to take good care of her relationship with a man like that."

As far as Helma knew, her mother had never exchanged a single word with Chief Gallant.

"The murderer might still be at large, you know," Helma said to distract her mother from her obvious train of thought.

"He's in Mexico or Canada by now," Lillian responded with certainty. "No murderer in his right mind would hang around here."

"I think murderers have stayed at the scene of the crime many times. Supposedly, it calls attention away from oneself."

"But only if you're from the town where you committed the murder," Lillian said around the last piece of dill pickle. "If you don't belong in the community, the best thing to do is to hightail it out of town. That's what I'd do anyway."

Helma finished her tea. The sun had broken through the clouds and beat against the side of her face. She raised her arms slightly away from her body so she wouldn't perspire on her blouse. Perhaps the window table hadn't been such a fortunate place to sit after all.

"Some people don't have an ounce of patience," Lillian was saying.

"What do you mean?"

"Look at that man," her mother said, nodding toward the window. "There are only two people ahead of him and he couldn't stand to wait a few more minutes. He looked at our table like we should just get right up and leave."

Helma squinted out the window at the man leaving Saul's Deli. He wore a blue suit and carried a notebook.

"Excuse me, Mother. I'll be right back."

Helma squeezed past the two people by the door and ran out onto the sidewalk, gasping as a skateboarder careened between her and a parking meter.

The man in the blue suit hastily climbed into the driver's side of a blue Ford. She was sure it was the same man who'd asked for college information, who'd dropped his notebook on her desk just before the yellow slip of paper disappeared.

"Sir!" she called.

She wasn't more than twenty feet from his car. He had to have heard her. But he slammed his car door and started the engine without a backward glance. He pulled into the traffic, wheels spinning, veering sharply in front of a bleating Volkswagen. Helma memorized his license plate number.

"What was that all about?" Lillian asked as Helma sat down again.

Helma took a pen from her purse and jotted the license plate number on the piece of notepaper where she'd written the letters and numbers from the yellow scrap. Her mother watched curiously.

"I think he was a patron who left something in the library," Helma explained. "I wanted to let him know we have it. Now what were you saying about getting away with murder?"

Lillian laughed. "Getting away with murder. That sounds like one of your father's weak jokes. I see they have some yummy-looking chocolate cheesecake at the counter. Let's split a piece."

"No thanks, Mother."

"A third?"

"Not for me, but you go ahead."

"Oh no, I could never eat a whole piece," Lillian said, looking soft-eyed toward the counter.

"I talked to Aunt Em last night," Helma told her mother.

Lillian fussed with her scarf. "And was Emily her happy, sunshiny self?"

"She seemed to be."

"*Mmmm.*"

"Why don't you two get along?" Helma asked.

"Why? What did she say?"

"Nothing. But it's obvious. It always has been."

Lillian shrugged. "Chemistry, I guess. Your father thought she was holy womanhood personified."

"She *was* his big sister," Helma reminded her.

"That family," Lillian said, shaking her head, warming up. "They were like a tornado, the way they sucked everybody up. Marrying into it was like joining the Mafia. Forget your own life; become an honorary Lithuanian. I'm half-Lithuanian myself but *my* family got over it. There you and Bruce and John were: *my* children, speaking Lithuanian before you were three."

"I only remember a few words now," Helma said.

"You'd probably still be speaking it if they hadn't started dying off the way they did," Lillian said. "*That* caught their attention."

Six children and Aunt Em was the only one left. Helma's father had been the last to die: dropping dead of a heart attack in the doctor's office three years ago. Helma had taken a week off and flown home to

Michigan in a confusing blur. She had a vague but doubtful memory of weeping in the arms of the cookie factory executive seated next to her on the plane.

The funeral was another vague blur, filled with the headachy odors of flowers and faces Helma could barely remember. Presiding over it all was that deeply dark, brass-handled casket. Two days later, when her brothers and their families had returned to Iowa and Grand Rapids, Helma flew back to Bellehaven. Once inside her apartment, she'd gone directly to bed and slept for twenty-one hours straight, waking famished, desperate to use the bathroom, and feeling as if her father's death was behind her.

"I suppose Emily told you the news," Helma's mother was saying.

"What? What news?"

Helma's mother bit her lip again and tapped the edge of her coffee cup. "Ricky's engaged."

"Ricky? Ricky who? You don't mean Uncle Mick's Ricky?"

"Of course."

"Cousin Ricky's engaged to be *married*?"

Lillian unwrapped the napkin filled with bread crusts and pulled one out. She studied it, shrugged apologetically, and bit the crust in half. "I know how you feel about Ricky, dear. All those silly little spats you two had over the years."

"They weren't 'silly little spats,' Mother. And I don't believe you do know how I feel. Ricky is a . . . Well, who ever consented to marry him?"

"She's young, I understand. One of the Cameron girls from outside Scoop River. A nurse's aide, or maybe it was a waitress. Something like that."

"I see."

Cousin Ricky was as close to being an enemy as a relative could get. Spoiled, selfish, egotistical, loud, a tormentor. Thirty-six years old and still living with his mother back in Scoop River, Michigan. Helma had endured being in the same class with him for thirteen years, "watching her back," as Ruth liked to say, waiting for Ricky to thwart her any way he could.

"Be nice to Ricky," Helma had grown up hearing. All because of the way his father, Helma's father's brother, had died when Ricky—and Helma—were nine.

In one brief moment Uncle Mick had given Ricky an excuse for every shortcoming he cared to exhibit the rest of his life.

"You should be happy for Ricky, Helma," Lillian said. "After all, he's thirty-six years old and never been married."

Helma ignored the pointed remark. "He might have if he'd left home."

"Don't be unkind, Helma. He wanted me to be sure and tell you about his engagement. He always asks after you and Ruth."

There'd been a fistfight in the back of the band room in ninth grade: Ruth and Ricky, after Ricky'd teased Ruth once too often about her height. Ruth had nearly won.

"I'll tell her."

"And how *is* Ruth these days?" Lillian asked, with a throaty edge to her voice.

"Ruth is . . . Ruth," Helma told her. "Busy at her art, a little intense, as always."

"I can't understand what people see in her paintings. It all looks like kindergarten art gone wild to me."

"She works very hard at it," Helma said noncommittally.

"I know she's your friend, dear, but the way she lives! It's hard to see what you two have in common. *You've* always been such a good girl. Those loud clothes; you'd think an artist would have better taste. And all the men she's seen with." Lillian shook her head, going "tch, tch," through her teeth, watching Helma expectantly.

Lillian said she couldn't stand gossip. "I only listen to facts," she was fond of saying, "not rumors." But

Helma noticed her mother dedicated a lot of energy to working her way through the rumors until she found the "facts."

Helma glanced at her watch. "I'd better be going back, Mother. I have a lot of work to do."

"Oh, my campaign posters! I wanted your opinion."

Lillian was running for president of the women's group in her retirement complex.

"Can I see them on Sunday?"

"Lillian!" a voice called as they made their way to the door.

"Catherine!"

A woman with snow-white hair sat at the table in the opposite window. Her hair was pulled back in a tight knot. Helma glanced at Catherine curiously. She'd read in a woman's magazine that when a woman pulled her hair back with a taut hold, she effectively pulled wrinkles out of her face.

"This is my daughter, Wilhelmina," Lillian said. "She's a librarian at the public library."

"How nice to meet you, Wilhelmina," Catherine said, shaking Helma's hand with a soft grip, smelling of lavender.

When Helma first graduated from library school, people used to say on meeting her, "But you don't look like a librarian!" Now, no one even blinked in surprise when they learned about her career. Helma attributed it to changing times; librarians weren't the stereotypes they once were.

"Wilhelmina was just telling me about the murder in the library," Lillian told Catherine.

Catherine clucked and shook her head. "Who'd have thought such a thing could take place in our library?"

"Certainly not the victim, I'm sure," Helma said. She patted her mother's arm. "I have to return to work now, Mother. It was nice to meet you, Catherine."

"Good-bye, dear. Say hello to Chief Gallant for me."

Catherine's eyebrows rose. One point for Lillian.

* * *

"Are these here for me to reshelve, Miss Zukas?" Patty asked Helma, pointing to the book truck Helma had been using for withdrawn books. "We need the truck."

"No, it's a project I'm working on. Let me have it for ten minutes more and I'll give it back to you."

Helma wheeled the book truck through the fiction aisles, across the new piece of carpeting and into the nonfiction 650s, all the while critically eyeing the alignment of the books, which shelves needed dusting or new bookends, which were too crowded.

Helma worked swiftly, guessing accurately more often than not which books hadn't circulated in three years. Mr. Upman had certainly let the system lapse.

Here was a title: *A multi-structural, multi-dimensional view of organizational behavior: a plan for the seventies.* A definite tosser. Helma pulled the green book from the shelf and opened the cover to the date due slip.

That was odd: it hadn't been checked out once in over four years and yet it had been checked out four times in the past year, the last two due dates were as recent as March 24 and April 21, only within the past two months.

Helma scanned the chapter headings. It looked deadly boring. Curious, she set it on her book truck to look at later. Maybe organizational behavior was about to become a hot topic in the business world.

She glanced up to see Patty awkwardly balancing an armload of books while she tried to reshelve. "You need this book truck more than I do," Helma told her. "I'll get rid of these and it's all yours."

She pushed the book truck into Jack the janitor's closet. The closet was actually a room as large as Mr. Upman's office, filled with supplies and a tattered easy chair in the corner, behind boxes of bathroom tissue. In one wall was a door to the incinerator shaft.

Helma pulled out the book cards, opened the door,

and pushed in the first three books, wincing as they tumbled down the shaft.

She hated to burn any book but other methods for getting rid of withdrawn books didn't seem to work. Whether they donated them to schools or nursing homes, sold them at book sales or sent them to the recyclers, the books always found their way back to the library. Earnestly and proudly handed back or slid down the book drop. People just couldn't believe that the WITHDRAWN stamp meant what it said.

Helma pushed the truck back to the circulation desk and took the organizational behavior book to her own desk in the workroom.

She glanced across the shelves that divided their spaces to be sure Patrice wasn't at her desk to overhear, then phoned Polly, the senior secretary in the police department.

"I was just going to call you and ask you to put Danielle Steel's new book on hold for me," Polly said when she heard Helma's voice.

Polly and Helma sometimes shared a lunch table in the city employees' dining room. Polly made up lists of romance novels and Helma pulled the books from the shelves and put them on hold so Polly could dash over on her break and pick them up. Helma hadn't read a romance since she was in eighth grade, and then only one: *Love's Passionate Remembrance*. She still blushed when she thought about Daphne and Roderick, and their troubled, tumultuous pursuit of one another.

"I'd be happy to. Could you possibly give me some advice?"

"Advice?" Polly laughed. "I'm not sure I'm qualified, but try me."

"There's been a car parked in my parking space at my apartment building the last few nights. I don't want to make trouble by complaining to the landlord. Could you find out who the license number belongs to so I could call the owner myself?"

"Sure. Just give me the number."

Helma read the number she'd taken from the car outside Saul's Deli. "HRZ 417."

"I'll call you back in a couple of minutes," Polly told her.

Helma wasn't scheduled for reference duty again the rest of the day, so she settled at her desk in the crowded workroom with last month's statistics on the number and kinds of reference questions the librarians had answered, and prepared to tally the columns of hatch marks. Mr. Upman would then pass the figures on to the library board, using them as evidence for badly needed new reference books.

Helma looked up to see Mr. Upman and Patrice enter the workroom together. Patrice's lips were tight. She went straight to her desk, busily fussing through a handful of papers without looking at Helma. Mr. Upman stopped beside Helma's desk.

"I hear you've been weeding the collection," he said, more with a trace of peevishness than authority.

"It's badly in need of it," Helma told him. There was total silence from Patrice's area. "Our shelves are overcrowded with books our patrons DO read. Imagine what would happen if for some reason everyone returned their books at once."

"Yes, yes. Total pandemonium."

"That isn't the word I'd choose but it certainly would be a problem."

"I hope you set aside the withdrawn books for donation to charity."

"I incinerated them. All but one I'd like to take a closer look at."

"Perhaps you'd forgotten I'd asked the staff not to weed the collection," Mr. Upman said. "Decisions to alter the general collection should be left to the director."

Helma's father had once told her: "Never admit you're wrong, Billie. Once you do, people start to believe it."

"I made my decisions with our patrons' interests in mind," Helma told him.

"I hope you won't, but should you take it upon yourself to weed the collection again, Miss Zukas, I'd prefer the withdrawn material be saved."

"It always finds its way back."

"We can donate it to less fortunate institutions than our own."

"Then they should be *distant* institutions," Helma reminded him.

Her phone buzzed and she picked it up, waiting until Mr. Upman backed away from her desk before she spoke into the receiver. It was Polly.

"I'm afraid this won't help you much, Helma," she said. "The car is a rental from Seattle. You'll probably have to make a complaint to your landlord after all."

"At least it's not one of my neighbors," Helma told her. "Thank you, Polly."

A rented car. It didn't mean anything. The man in the blue suit simply might not have heard her call him, with the traffic noises. He might *not* have rushed out of Saul's Deli because he recognized Helma. He might not have taken the yellow scrap of paper. Why would he want it, anyway?

Helma stood to go check out the behavior organization book and absentmindedly bumped a box of books.

"Oh!" she said aloud.

"Are you all right?" Barbara, who was labeling books across the room, asked.

"Fine, thank you. I caught my heel on one of these boxes."

"I'm not surprised. We're too crowded back here."

Helma didn't answer. It was a common refrain from the staff. Not enough room. Elbow to elbow. Stacks of books and materials where there should be organized shelves and cabinets. Not enough room; not enough money. Simply not enough.

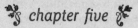

EVENING
AT HOME

Helma switched on the talk radio station as she drove home.

"Is it true?" the announcer was asking. "Do you think there's an anomaly in some people's genetic makeup that makes them unsuitable for marriage? Call me. Let's talk about it."

She punched the button for the easy listening station and sat back in the driver's seat, humming along inside her head to "Strangers in the Night."

So cousin Ricky was getting married. The word "anomaly" did come to mind. She'd withhold her belief until Aunt Em sent her an account of the wedding from the Scoop River paper.

She slowed her Buick behind a bicyclist riding five feet into the lane. Helma hadn't ridden a bicycle since elementary school but she certainly remembered how automobiles had whizzed past her so dangerously close back then. She sympathized with the cyclists' demands for more bike lanes.

Of course she'd never known anyone who wore clothing comparable to the leotard-like suit the rider in front of her—and a lot of bicyclists—wore now. You could see his thigh muscles tense and release through it, and probably more than that if a driver had the time or the interest to look.

She glanced into her rearview mirror and noted the line of cars forced to slow behind her. The driver of the car directly in back of her shook his fist and Helma dropped her speed from fifteen to thirteen miles per hour.

Mrs. Whitney in 3E tapped on her window, motioning to Helma. Helma waved and waited for Mrs. Whitney to come to her door.

Helma was one of the youngest dwellers in Bayside Arms. Fourteen years ago, when she rented her apartment, there was also an opening in Gullview Apartments. The view was actually better at Gullview but at Gullview they allowed families with children.

"I'm so glad I caught you, Helma," Mrs. Whitney said. "I just got a new little darling I want you to see."

Mrs. Whitney was a plump, white-haired widow whose daughters lived in California. She wore Mother Hubbard aprons and sturdy shoes and baked more than she could eat.

Helma glanced at her watch and Mrs. Whitney patted her shoulder. "Only take a second, darlin'. I've got some nice fresh banana bread for you to take home for your supper, too."

A rainbow of pastel dolls, crocheted doilies, knitted afghans, framed stitchwork, and hooked rugs filled Mrs. Whitney's apartment. Hundreds of tiny little eyes stared aimlessly about from shelves and tables and chairs. Dimpled cheeks and chubby lips vacantly grinned into the room.

"Here he is," Mrs. Whitney said. "Doesn't he just break your heart?"

On Mrs. Whitney's coffee table, next to silk roses in a basket weave china vase, a porcelain baby boy sat on a potty chair and gleefully unfurled a very tiny roll of bathroom tissue.

"It's amazing they can create skin tones like that," Helma said.

"Isn't it though? You'd think he was about to get right up and wipe his little pink bum, wouldn't you?"

Helma didn't think so at all, but she quickly asked, "Where did you find him?"

"In the magazine section of the Sunday paper," Mrs. Whitney said. "He just arrived this morning."

"He's certainly an addition to your collection."

"Thank you." Mrs. Whitney gently stroked the porcelain doll's cheek, smiling fondly. "Did you have a hard day? Everybody's talking about that murder."

"It was a shock," Helma told her.

"Such a shame. It's not safe anywhere, is it? Not even in your own home. I feel safer knowing you're just on the other side of my wall, I'll tell you that." Mrs. Whitney squeezed Helma's arm. "Now let me get that banana bread so you can get home and kick off your shoes and relax."

Helma broiled a salmon steak for dinner. She placed a generous pat of real butter on the salmon, and a pat of butter on her green beans, and another pat on a split and warmed white dinner roll. She dined facing the bay, with her back to the kitchen.

A gleaming white ferry headed for the islands, a line of passengers standing along its deck. It had been almost a year since Helma had ridden the ferries. Maybe next weekend, if it was nice. Sailboats and wind surfers crossed her view, as Northwesterners took advantage of the sudden sunshine. Farther out, a tugboat towed a barge of golden sawdust away from the lumber mill across the bay. Still farther out, the San Juan Islands slipped into deep shadow as the sun lowered.

On any other night Helma would have sat and enjoyed the setting sun highlighting the comings and goings on the bay. But tonight she took the piece of notepaper that duplicated the letters and numbers on the yellow slip and opened it flat on her linen place mat.

The letters made no sense: SQ VILKE HRC. She examined the dates: Mar. 10 and April 7, a month apart; and the two sets of four numbers: "1469 or 1649." They might be part of an address. It could be a house number on any street in Bellehaven.

Or perhaps it was the last four digits of a phone number. Helma idly wrote down the local telephone exchanges: 623, 676, 606, 612. Just four of them.

She rolled and unrolled the edge of her place mat between her fingers, studying the notepaper with its letters and numbers and the license plate number, wondering if somehow there was a connection between the man who'd dropped his notebook on her desk and the yellow slip of paper, and the murdered man who'd been using the city directory from which the yellow slip of paper had fallen. What if it had been *his* paper?

But why would he leave it in the city directory? He'd been intent on searching the directory, not at all like someone who would forget to take his information away with him.

Helma tapped her pencil, first the eraser, then the point, back and forth, thudding it against her place mat. The sun dipped behind the islands and she continued to tap.

What if, just supposing, the murdered man hadn't accidentally forgotten the yellow paper, that instead he'd *hidden* the slip of information in the city directory, intending to return and retrieve it later?

Helma saw she was making a lead smudge on her linen place mat and leaned forward to set the pencil out of her reach.

Why hide the paper in the directory when he could as easily have slipped it into his pocket? Unless, he'd been *forced* to hide the paper. What if he saw someone watching him or following him, someone he was afraid of, someone who could make sense of the seemingly meaningless letters and numbers? Perhaps the man in the suit?

She should inform Chief Gallant. Helma moved the telephone from the kitchen counter to the dining table. She took Chief Gallant's card from her pocket and pushed the buttons of his home number.

"Hello?"

It was a woman. Whatever his personal situation might be, it was none of Helma's concern.

"May I speak to Chief Gallant, please?" Helma asked.

"May I ask who's calling?" the woman asked in cool tones.

"It's a police matter," Helma told her.

"Oh. He's at the office. I can take a message."

"Tell him . . ." She paused. "No, it won't be necessary. I'll phone his office."

She replaced the phone on its cradle. What could she tell him? That she'd lost a yellow piece of paper that made no sense and might or might not have belonged to the murdered man and might or might not have been taken by a man who might not have a college-age son? What could she say about the man in the rented car, that he didn't stop when a woman he didn't know called to him, that he pulled out suspiciously fast into traffic?

Helma smoothed the slip of paper and dismissed the idea of calling the chief. Her conjectures were hardly substantial enough to disrupt his work.

She again studied the possible phone numbers and exchanges. What if she called the numbers? There was no reason to. But then there was no reason not to, either.

Helma dialed the first exchange: 623, with the first set of numbers: 1469. It rang.

"Hello?" answered the low-throated voice of a woman who Helma immediately suspected was a heavy smoker.

Helma hadn't planned what to say.

"Hello?" the woman repeated, irritation edging her voice.

"Yes," Helma said briskly. "This is your public library calling. We recently found a personal letter in one of our books and we think this telephone number is on it. It's smudged so it's difficult to tell, but we wanted to phone you to inquire if you'd lost a letter."

Helma pressed her forehead with her other hand, shaking her head. Who'd believe such a weak excuse?

"How kind of you to go to this much trouble," the woman said, her voice warming. "but I'm sure it's not mine. I'm not missing any letters that I know of. Who's the letter addressed to?"

"The envelope's missing. It begins, 'Dear Betty.' "

"No, it's not anyone here. Thank you for calling though."

The next two phone numbers greeted her with the mechanical man chastising her, "Your call cannot be completed as dialed. Please check your directory and dial again. If your call still cannot be completed, please dial directory assistance."

A man answered the 623-1469 number. Helma only had time to say, "This is your public library," before he guffawed and said, "Library! Hell, I don't even know where the library is."

"It's directly across from the police station, which you no doubt *are* aware of," Helma said, and hung up.

Helma started on the next four-digit set, repeating the four exchanges. The first one, 623-1649, rang but went unanswered. The next one, 676-1649, was answered by a man.

"Yes?" he queried quietly, rather than answering with the customary hello.

After Helma told him about the letter found in the library, there was a click followed by silence. It wasn't like the sound of a receiver being hung up, but more of a metallic click.

"Hello," Helma said. "Are you still there?"

There was no reply.

"Please come to the library reference desk to claim the letter if it belongs to you," Helma said into the eerie silence and hung up.

The last two numbers were again answered by recordings urging Helma to get her dialing habits straightened out. Helma retrieved her pencil and listed the eight possible telephone numbers. She crossed out four of them, printed "no answer" by two of them, "pleasant woman" by 623-1469, "rude man" by 612-1649, and "answer without acknowledgment" by 676-1649. It wasn't much and it meant nothing.

Dusky purple shaded the undersides of a string of clouds across the sky. The last of the boats, pale lights winking on their bows, made a wavering line back to the lighted docks of the marina. Helma turned over her notepaper and began a grocery list: window cleaner, lettuce . . .

Her phone rang.

"Hello?" Helma said.

Silence.

"Hello?" Helma said in her silver-dime voice. "May I help you?"

No answer. She held the receiver close to her ear, listening. She didn't hear any heavy breathing, no background sounds either. Just dense silence, thick expectant stillness. Then there was another sound, a soft click.

Helma dropped the phone back on its cradle, killing the connection. Then for no reason, she looked over her shoulder, behind her.

Although it was Friday and Helma had taken a shower that morning, she immersed herself in a long, hot bath, relaxing her head on the inflatable seashell pillow. In her mind, she pictured a blank piece of light blue paper that securely separated her from murders and strangers and cryptic notes. The phone rang but she ignored it and after five rings it quit.

When her bathwater began to cool, Helma climbed out and spread an odorless moisturizing lotion from the soles of her feet to the base of her chin. Then she put on her nightgown and robe and went to the kitchen to fix a cup of caffeine-free tea.

The fluorescent tube over the stove made the room bright enough to see while she put on the kettle and got out a cup and tea bag.

A soft thud sounded outside her apartment door. Helma turned and looked at the windowless door, pulling her robe tighter.

If it was another cat, she was calling the manager, no matter what time it was. Animals weren't allowed at Bayside Arms; it was right there in black and white in her lease. Helma had her suspicions about the bundle she'd seen the couple in 2D carrying in and out of their apartment.

Her outside light was off and someone had probably bumped into her door in the dark. She hoped he or she hadn't tripped on her pot of daisies.

She was turning back to the stove when from the corner of her eye she saw the doorknob turn. Slowly. Clockwise.

Helma froze, her breath held, watching in horror.

Was the door locked? Her mind went blank. Hadn't she locked it when she came home? She couldn't remember. She must have; she never even took out the garbage without locking the door and carrying her keys with her.

And then, just as slowly, the doorknob turned the other way, stealthily, deliberately.

Helma took a step toward the door, then a step back. *Go look through the peephole*, she told herself. *See who it is. Get a description for the police.* Go do it. Now.

Suddenly from behind her the teakettle burst into a furious whistle. Helma jumped and grabbed for it. Hot steam blasted against her wrist and she couldn't help it; she dropped the silver kettle and it tipped and fell, clattering to the floor. Boiling water spewed across the patterned tile.

Helma leapt out of the steaming water's path and rushed to the door. She flicked on the outdoor light and pressed her eye against the peephole.

All she saw through the telescope-like lens was her cocoa doormat and the flowerpots of daisies. No other sound reached her ears. No desperate clambering of someone escaping down the three flights of steps, no car squealing into the street.

Helma stood with her eye to the peephole for long minutes. Not moving, barely breathing, her eye watering. There was nothing suspicious. No one was there.

Finally she rechecked the lock, tested the dead bolt, and turned back to her kitchen.

"Dante's donuts," she said.

Water pooled in a glimmering sheet across the floor. The teakettle rested on its side against the counter's mop board, steamy water still dripping from its spout.

She pulled up the woven rug in front of the sink and threw a dish towel on the floor, making a dam to stop the water from spreading beneath the counter. She tore open a new package of sponges and threw them on the floor, too.

When the mess was finally cleaned up, Helma checked the peephole one more time. The night was dark and silent.

She put the kettle under the faucet to refill it. The stream of water missed the spout, splattering over the sides of the kettle onto Helma's arm. She stared at the kettle, puzzled, then at her hands. They were shaking.

Helma left the kettle in the sink, shoved her hands into the pockets of her robe, and went to bed.

❧ chapter six ❧

MISS ZUKAS
RESCUES RUTH

By the time Helma realized she wasn't dreaming, her telephone had rung at least six times. She rose on her elbows and peered at the red digital numbers on her clock radio.

1:47.

"Yes?" she inquired. Polite but cold. One forty-seven in the morning!

"Helm! What are you doing?"

It was Ruth. Naturally.

"I *was* doing exactly what you should be doing: sleeping."

Ruth giggled and Helma knew instantly that Ruth was intoxicated.

"It's Friday night, Helma. You should be out playing, not sleeping the whole goddamn weekend away."

Helma maintained her silence. She'd discovered years ago that silence was frequently the most effective way to deal with Ruth. Ruth relished a quarrel; she bloomed in battle, enthusiastically teasing and toying with anyone who pleaded with her for more reasonable behavior. But the silence of no response left Ruth confused and uncertain and ripe for conquest.

"Sleep, sleep, sleep," Ruth muttered into the phone. "Have you fallen asleep already? Still there?" she asked, her voice so piercing that Helma pulled the receiver away from her ear.

"I'm still here, Ruth. If you phoned to chat, I'd like to save it for another time, if you don't mind."

"Oh, Helm. Dear, dear Helmie. Don't hang up. Ruthie's got herself into a bit of a jam."

"What have you done, Ruth?" Helma turned on the bedside lamp and pulled the covers up over her shoulders. This could be a long conversation.

"I haven't *done* anything, Helm dearest," Ruth said in alcoholic indignation. "I accidentally fell into a situation from which I had the wisdom to foresee it was best to extricate myself."

"And what would you like me to do?" Helma asked.

Ruth's voice lowered, cajoled. "If you could just come pick me up and take me home. That's all. Nothing to it."

"Where's your car?"

There was silence, and then after a drawn out sigh, Ruth said, "I don't know."

"Oh, Ruth."

"But I'm sure that in the morning it'll all be clear to me. I just can't think right now."

In the background, Helma heard the moan of a train whistle. It was loud, as if Ruth were only feet away from it.

"Where on earth are you?"

"Down at Squabbly Harbor near that new little restaurant with a view of the marina. You know?"

Helma did know. A mixture of light industry, waterfront development, a train switching yard, a marina of fishing and recreational boats. Not very well lit and no residences for blocks. She'd heard there was an old-style hobo camp close to the train yard. Helma doubted it was a very safe place to be after dark.

"Ruth, are you alone?"

"Yes," Ruth admitted.

"Now listen to me."

There was silence.

"Are you listening to me, Ruth?" Helma asked.

"Yes, Helma."

"Stay right where you are, right beside the pay phone. Do you have another quarter? No, never mind. That doesn't matter. I'll be right down to pick you up. If you need help before I get there, if you even *think* you're in danger, dial 911. You won't need a quarter. Just dial 911." Helma spoke in a distinct, evenly modulated voice. "Nine-one-one. Do you promise?"

"Nine-one-one," Ruth promised earnestly, gratefully. "I promise."

Helma hung up and folded back the bed covers.

"Oh, Faulkner," she said as she pulled the hairnet from her head and fluffed her hair with her fingers.

This wasn't the first time she'd had to assist Ruth out of some mess. It wasn't at all unusual for Ruth to show up panic-stricken on Helma's doorstep when she was up to something she had reason to regret. It had started long ago.

When they were seventeen, Ruth had desperately phoned Helma on Prom night at 2:30 in the morning, begging her to pick her up on the shore of Lake Michigan. Luckily, Helma had been up reading a new political thriller and had grabbed the phone before her mother or father heard it. She'd sneaked out—for the only time in her life—taking her parents' car and slowly driving along the shore until her headlights picked out a bedraggled Ruth sitting on the side of a sand dune. Drunk, her dress torn, and the boy gone off in his car with a black eye.

There was the July night Ruth's derelict Saab broke down with fifty pounds of fresh salmon that she'd received in trade for a painting in the trunk. And what about the time Helma had loaned Ruth the fine money after she'd joined that demonstration?

But Helma would be the first—and not without gratitude—to acknowledge that it wasn't one-sided. She remembered the night Ruth had sat up with her after Helma and Patrice had fought over the new microfiche machines. Helma had wanted to quit her job and go back to Michigan. The night Helma's father died, Ruth had broken every speed limit to drive her a hundred miles to the airport in Seattle for a late flight, and then had to pay seventy-five dollars to get her car out of hock after it had been towed because Helma's plane was late after all and Ruth had refused to leave Helma alone to go park it legally. And long, long ago, there'd been that letter from Donald about the girl he'd met at the University of Connecticut. Helma briefly closed her eyes; she couldn't think about *that*.

Despite this, whenever they spent longer than an hour together, Helma began to feel as frustrated as if she were stuck in an enclosed area with an irate baby. She wasn't sure how Ruth felt but she had noticed that just about the time Helma was searching for an excuse to part company, Ruth was puffing her cheeks and tapping her foot to an unrecognizable rhythm.

She thumbed through her closet. Helma's clothes hung by category and color. First her short-sleeved blouses, beginning with a white sleeveless top and ending with a navy blue silk, then her long-sleeved blouses and turtlenecks, followed by skirts, pants, and dresses. She chose appropriate night clothes: a blue pullover turtleneck and a pair of black slacks, and a navy sweater that buttoned up the front. She didn't have time to put on lipstick or do more than fluff her hair; who knew what danger Ruth was in?

The streets of Bellehaven at two in the morning were unfamiliar, like one of those gaudy surrealist paintings that Ruth liked, with the pavement glistening too black, the light too defined, and the shadows too thick. A silvery mist hovered above the orange streetlights like a vaporous ceiling.

Helma checked her windows and locked the car doors from the inside and when she passed a bearded man shuffling along the boulevard with a bulging plastic garbage bag over his shoulder, she resolutely looked away.

A few cars were out; all of them seemed to be black and traveling inordinately fast. One car stopped opposite her at a red light and then zoomed through it, squealing around the corner, a quick image of too many young men.

Somewhere out here, whoever had been at her door was going about his nefarious business, lurking in the dark, maybe testing the locks on another innocent victim's home.

Helma kept her eyes on the street ahead of her, looking neither left nor right, with no intention of making eye contact with the elements that frequented these hours.

The avenue down to Squabbly Harbor stretched broad and empty in front of her. Helma drove her car through the round spotlights made by mercury vapor lamps. Directly to her right, the train switching yard was filled with the rumble and metal screeches of train cars being dropped from or added to other trains. The cars jolted and banged together, moaning iron against steel. No sign of humans, as if the trains were being operated by remote control—or by phantoms.

" 'The gingham dog and the calico cat,' " she recited aloud, " 'side by side on the table sat.' " She finished with " 'And that is how I came to know' " and properly added the credit, "Eugene Field." She was on the second stanza of "The Owl and the Pussycat" when she reached Squabbly Harbor.

She turned into the feebly lit parking lot by the sprawling buildings that housed the cafe and a few shops, built in the manner popularized by Californians: redwood siding, baskets of flowers hanging under the eaves, a deck courtyard. A pickup and a station wagon, which she hoped were both empty, were parked at the far end by the Dumpsters.

Helma pulled her car close to the courtyard where two pay phones were attached to the wall, their fluorescent logos blooming in the shadows. It was obvious Ruth wasn't waiting next to the pay phones as she'd promised.

Helma wasn't about to honk her car horn, but she tactfully pressed the gas pedal three times, racing the motor. Ruth still didn't appear. Nothing moved in the darkness.

Finally, Helma squeezed her purse under the seat, removed her keys from the ignition, and stepped out of the car, locking the door behind her.

A damp breeze drifted up from the water, carrying the odors of salt and seaweed. From the marina below came the singing of hardware against metal, pealing like bells, accompanied by the whispers of water nudging against boats and pilings. In the daylight, a stroll along the complicated arrangement of docks to look at the boats was one of her favorite walks. Now they were only a mass of unsettling shadows and outlines. Helma crossed her arms, pulling her sweater more tightly around her and climbed the steps toward the pay phones.

"Ruth?" she called into the darkness, her voice hoarse, like a whisper.

Helma looped the key ring over her thumb and held her keys inside her fist as she'd been taught in self-defense class.

She peered cautiously into the murky shadows before she took each step that carried her farther into the darkness of the buildings, steadying herself with her hand against the rough cedar walls.

"Ruth?" she called again.

"Mmm?" came lazily from the left.

A form lay stretched on one of the planked wooden benches built into the side of the building. Helma stepped closer and recognized Ruth raising herself on one elbow, her hair undone and bushed around her face.

"Helm, is that you?"

"Helma," Helma corrected automatically.

"Whatever," Ruth mumbled, rising unsteadily to a sitting position. "You're a peach to come down here and rescue bad old Ruthie."

"Why don't we just get in the car now, Ruth." Helma gripped Ruth's arm under her elbow and pulled her up from the bench.

Ruth stood awkwardly, leaning heavily against Helma, one arm across Helma's shoulder.

"Where's your shoe?" Helma asked, stopping when she realized that Ruth was walking, staggering really, like a peg-legged cartoon character.

Ruth looked down at her feet: one scuffed two-inch boot and the other shoeless foot. She turned the stockinged foot from side to side, admiring it.

"I do believe that man still has it." She giggled and hugged Helma's shoulders. "It should just about fit him, too."

Helma turned her car keys out of her fist and unlocked the passenger door, steering Ruth inside, pulling her skirt out of the door before she closed it. Walking around to the driver's side, she felt the empty darkness around them, punctuated by the screeching, switching trains and the chiming from the marina. It was a lonely place. Where were all the security guards the harbor was so quick to boast about?

Ruth sprawled in the front seat, her long legs splayed out under the dashboard and her head on the headrest.

"Put on your seat belt, please," Helma reminded her.

Ruth laughed. "Riding with you is safer than a baby in its tender loving mother's arms. A seat belt would be redundant."

"At least lock your door."

Ruth reached behind her and Helma waited until she heard the click of the lock before she started the car and gladly pulled out of the empty parking lot.

"Oh, Helm. I can't believe how stupid I can be sometimes. I was at this party and this man—I'd never seen him before, from San Francisco or New York or somewhere populated—asked to take me home." Ruth leaned her head against the door window, lolling. "I never thought I'd fall for that one. I'm thirty-seven years old, for Chrissake. He . . ."

"I really don't care to hear about it, Ruth," Helma told her, taking her eyes off the street for a second to meet Ruth's.

"Yeah," Ruth agreed. "It's not such a great story."

After a few minutes of silence as Helma navigated the car back through town toward Ruth's south side house, Ruth tapped Helma's shoulder.

"Had the craziest dream. It felt so real I knew I had to be skunk drunk. I was waiting for you, just like I really was, and all of a sudden my father was there, just standing in front of me, looking at me, with his hands on his hips. The little twit puffed himself all up like he used to when he thought he was being tough, and said, 'Stretch, you look like a goddamn drunken two-bit tart. I'm embarrassed and I'd be ashamed to be seen with you.'"

Ruth poked Helma's shoulder again and giggled. "You know what I said? I said, 'Then why don't you drop dead, you old fart?' 'Drop dead,' I said." She giggled again. " 'Drop dead.' And you know, that's exactly what he did. He lay down on the bench across from me, stretched himself out on his back, and folded his hands over his chest like he was in a casket, and poof, just disappeared. Then I woke up."

"Just how much did you drink, Ruth?" Helma asked.

Ruth pinched her thumb and forefinger together and then opened them an inch. "Only a little bit."

"Mmm," Helma commented.

"It won't change my life a rat's ass ounce if you don't believe me," Ruth said indignantly.

Then, in a flash her mood changed. She smiled. "Wasn't that a hilarious dream? I wonder why my old man was trying to play Daddy Dearest?"

"Only you can answer that," Helma said. "It was *your* dream."

"Oh, goody. Are you going to give me a lecture in pop psychobabble?"

Helma didn't answer. Ruth squirmed and sighed and looked out the window into the night. "Dead parents," she said. "Between the two of us all we've got left is your mother."

"But she knew all of them," Helma said.

Ruth laughed softly. "In a funny way, that counts for something, doesn't it? You're alive as long as you're remembered. You know, I heard a naughty little story once about your father and my mother. You know how emotional he was? It seems . . ."

"I won't listen to any gossip, Ruth," Helma said, "especially about the dead."

"I won't listen to any gossip, Ruth," Ruth mimicked in a stern falsetto and laid her head against her window.

Ruth lived in a tiny house off the alley between two stately Victorian homes on Spruce Street, on what was referred to as "the Slope." The Slope was graced by beautiful old homes that had once belonged to lumber and fishing magnates. The vegetation on the Slope was old and powerful and startlingly green, threatening to engulf in vines and creeping shrubbery any building that lay untended in its way.

Eighty years ago Ruth's house had been a carriage house. Ten blocks from Helma's apartment building, it nestled between old pines and willows and tall shrubs, with a partial view of the bay. Helma rarely visited Ruth's house. Once she'd tried to clean it as a surprise, and Ruth hadn't spoken to her for a month.

Helma parked in the middle of the narrow alley and turned off the engine.

"Now what?" Ruth asked.

"We're here."

"Where?"

"At your house."

"I guess I'll get out then." Ruth opened her door and the dome light came on.

"I think I'd better help you."

When she rounded the car to Ruth's side, Ruth held a book close to her face, squinting. "What's this, Helma, a little light reading? Maybe it's my state but I don't even understand the title."

It was the organizational behavior book.

"Some library homework. I forgot to bring it in my apartment."

"With good reason."

Helma steered Ruth down the steps to her front door.

"I can do it," Ruth said. "Want to come in and have a drink, or a cup of tea—if I have any?"

"No, thank you. I'd really prefer to get some sleep."

"Oh, Helmie. Why can't I be more like you? Tucked in by ten. Up and shining by seven. Clean underwear every morning. You are an ideal woman."

Ruth turned on the light in her kitchen–dining room. Helma winced at the stacks of mail and papers and unwashed dishes. In the combination living room–bedroom, she could see Ruth's strewn clothes and her unmade sofa bed. There was a bedroom, too, but Ruth had converted it into her studio.

The smell of oil paints and paint thinner wafted from Ruth's house into the still night air. "Death hours," her father had always called the time between 2:00 A.M. and 5.00 A.M. The period when the call came to tell you that your brother or your mother or your favorite uncle was dead.

"Will you be all right?" Helma asked.

"I will be until I wake up," Ruth said, touching her forehead. "The wages of sin, you know."

Ruth suddenly leaned down and hugged Helma. "Thanks, Helm. I'll make it up to you someday," she said.

"If so, I'm sure it'll be under far different circumstances," Helma told her.

Ruth laughed, swaying a little. "I'm sure it will be," she said. "Good night." And stood framed in the light of her open door, her hair brushing the lintel, until Helma got back up the steps to her car.

When Helma reached her apartment door, her telephone was ringing. She glanced at her watch: nearly two-thirty. Now what?

She opened her door, relocked it behind her, put on the dead bolt, set her purse and the book on the table, and took off her sweater. The phone still rang. She counted eight rings, and who knew how many more times it had rung before she got home?

"Hello?" she answered cautiously.

"Helma?"

It was Ruth.

"What's wrong now?" Helma asked.

"Nothing," came Ruth's voice, no longer slurred, just husky. "I wanted to be sure you made it home all right."

"Why wouldn't I have?" Helma asked.

"Well . . . that guy. Did he follow you?"

"What 'guy'?"

"There was this guy, I mean I think it was a guy. He was behind us from Squabbly Harbor. I watched you come out of the alley from my house onto the street, and not more than five seconds later, here he came, right after you. I'm sure it was the same car. Positive. I phoned your number and let it ring until you answered. It made me feel better, you know?"

"Why didn't you mention it when I was driving you home?"

"I thought maybe I was jumping to alcoholic delusions, until I saw him follow you from my house," Ruth said contritely. "Then I got worried."

"Did you see what kind of a car it was, or what he looked like?"

"Just a dark car, maybe black or navy, I don't know. A newer car, I think. Just a car."

"Did you see the license plate?"

"Helma!" Ruth whined. "The license plate! Not a chance. I'm in an alcoholic stupor, remember?"

"I'll look and see if there's a suspicious car outside the apartment building."

"No! Don't go outside! Call the police. What if he's a murderer or something? Just stay inside."

"If I see anything suspicious, I'll call the police."

Ruth yawned into the telephone. "You know what's best. Like you told me: dial 911."

"Good night, Ruth."

"G'night, Helm."

Helma hung up and went to her door. She placed her hand on the knob. She undid the dead bolt. Then she redid the bolt and pulled away her hand as if the doorknob were boiling hot, remembering how it had turned. Ruth was right; it was more prudent to look through a window first.

The window from her back bedroom had the clearest view of the parking lot. She left the lights off and cautiously pulled back the curtains, first checking the outside landing that stretched across each floor of the Bayside Arms. No dark cars idled in the drive; no leering faces peered up at her apartment. A van passed by on the boulevard. Not even a breeze stirred the wind sock mounted on the carports.

Of course, if someone *had* been following her, he wouldn't be foolish enough to be lounging around within view. Ruth had been inebriated. All cars looked alike in her state; it had only seemed to Ruth that they were being followed. Helma shook her head and stepped back from the window, pulling the curtains together so there wasn't any gap. What a night of paranoia!

She had to get back to bed. She was exhausted. Tomorrow was Saturday, but there was no sense in totally disrupting her circadian rhythms. Maybe a cup of hot milk would settle her mind.

Helma returned to the kitchen and turned on the overhead light. She froze in the middle of the room, her hand still poised over the light switch, frowning, tipping her head. Her nostrils flared.

Someone had been in her apartment. She could feel it. Still not moving, she swept her eyes around the kitchen and into the dining area.

Anyone not as careful as Helma Zukas might not have noticed that her hand-thrown pottery canister set was slightly out of line. The silverware drawer was just barely open; the damp rug she'd rolled up was askew. Her address book next to the telephone was not sitting flat on the counter, as if its pages had been turned and not smoothed neatly down again. She was positive she'd left her chairs pushed in, evenly spaced around her kitchen table.

Helma stood statue-still and listened, every sense knife-edge alert for an intruder to step forward and make demands for who-knew-what. Her apartment was death-hour silent, just the ticking of her grandmother's mantel clock and the gentle gurgle of freon circulating in her refrigerator.

Could the intruder still be in her apartment? In her bedroom? Her bathroom? Maybe even hidden in the back bedroom, where she'd missed him lurking in the darkness, watching her?

Helma edged toward the telephone on the kitchen counter, her oxfords noiseless on the vinyl floor. She lifted the receiver and quickly tapped out 911.

"What is your emergency?"

"This is Helma Zukas in 3F of the Bayside Arms. There's been an intruder in my apartment."

"Is he there now?"

"I don't think so, but I'm not certain."

"Don't hang up. The police are on their way. I'll stay on the line with you until they arrive. Try to remain calm. An officer will be there in a moment."

Helma listened to the droning voice without knowing what the woman was repeating, something about safe and calm. The longer she stood there the more she trusted her intuition that whoever had been inside had already made his escape. She couldn't "feel" an intruder.

Still holding the telephone to her ear, she stepped away from the kitchen counter and peered into her living room. At first she noticed nothing amiss; then she realized that her tweed throw pillow was on top instead of under the solid brown pillow. Books were not as neatly aligned on their shelves, and hadn't her magazines been straighter on the coffee table? She glanced down the hall toward her own bedroom door opposite the back bedroom. The door was shut just as she'd left it.

The muffled voice of the 911 operator answered a second call, leaving the line open so Helma could hear her calming instruction to another desperate person.

"Are you still there, Mrs. Zukas?"

"Miss," Helma corrected.

"Is everything still all right?"

"Yes, I'm fine. Thank you."

"A police officer is about a block from your apartment right now. He should arrive in a few seconds. I'll wait here with you."

A staccato rapping sounded on Helma's door. Obviously the police couldn't be bothered with the frivolity of doorbells.

"Someone's at my door now," Helma told the operator.

"Don't hang up," she instructed. "Lay the phone down and check to be sure it is a policeman before you open the door. Let me talk to him after you let him in."

Through the peephole in her door, Helma identified the blue uniform, a fishbowl distorted face level with her own. She unbolted the door.

"Ma'am," he said, touching his hat. "You've had a break-in?"

Helma recognized him as the officer whose police car had been parked in her slot on the morning of the murder. Sidney Lehman, his badge read. He was young, no more than twenty-five, still possessing a blond, unformed air. He showed no sign he remembered her.

After he identified himself to the 911 operator and hung up the phone, Helma explained briefly what had occurred.

"When did the break-in take place?" he asked.

"Between 1:50 and 2:30," Helma told him.

"And can you identify what was taken?"

"I haven't checked the other rooms yet, or made a thorough inventory."

"Excuse me," Officer Lehman said and drew his revolver, a brutish-looking piece that gleamed deadly black. Before he had taken two steps down her hall, another knock sounded at Helma's door. Helma and Officer Lehman looked at each other in surprise.

"Are you expecting anyone?" Officer Lehman asked.

"Not many people drop in at this time of night."

The officer opened her door, still holding his gun in his hand. Helma stepped back to the living room end of her kitchen.

"Chief," she heard Officer Lehman say.

"Sid," Chief Gallant said and stepped inside. The suit he'd worn when he questioned her in the library was rumpled and his collar stood open. Substantial dark circles pouched beneath his eyes. Helma doubted he'd been to bed yet.

The two policemen seemed to take up an unusual amount of room in her kitchen.

"Miss Zukas," the chief acknowledged. "I heard the call on my radio and came right over."

"You must not get much sleep if you respond to all your officers' calls."

Chief Gallant met Helma's eyes. "Not all calls, Miss Zukas. Just the ones I feel might be related to a case I'm working on."

"What case?" Then she remembered the murder. "Oh, do you mean the murder?"

Chief Gallant turned to Officer Lehman. "Go ahead and check the rest of the apartment."

When Officer Lehman had disappeared into the back bedroom, gun first, Chief Gallant took his spiral notebook from his pocket and asked, "Have you found anything missing?"

Helma shook her head.

"What was damaged?"

"Nothing really."

One of the chief's eyebrows raised. He held his pencil motionless over his paper.

"There were a few things out of order," Helma said, "not really tampered with, just disturbed." She pointed out the address book and the rug, the out-of-line magazines on her coffee table.

"Were you asleep?"

"No. It was necessary for me to leave the apartment at 1:47 A.M."

"May I ask why?"

"It's not a police concern, but a friend of mine was in a difficult situation and I gave her a ride home."

"Did you notice anyone loitering around the building when you left?"

Helma shook her head. For a brief moment she considered telling him what the inebriated Ruth had said about a car following her home. But no, that was a coincidence, Ruth's distorted imagination. "But earli-

er this evening someone tried to enter my apartment."
She described the turning doorknob and the teakettle.

The chief made notations in his notebook, nodding
as he wrote. "And you think it might be the same
person?"

"It seems likely, doesn't it?"

"Are you certain someone was at your door?"

"The doorknob didn't turn by itself," she told Chief
Gallant. "What does this have to do with the murder
at the library?"

Chief Gallant shrugged. "Probably nothing. It's my
office's practice to take an interest in what happens to
people in any way associated with another case. You
work at the library; you spoke with the victim; you
saw the body. So, therefore, you're associated with the
case."

"I see," Helma conceded. "Then you know something
more about the case?"

Helma couldn't have said what made her ask that. It
might have been that Chief Gallant seemed more confident than when she'd answered his questions in the
library, as if he had less of a mystery on his hands.

He scratched his head. "Well, I guess it'll be in the
paper tomorrow. The victim's name was Ernie Larsen.
He wasn't a transient but he was a man who moved
around a lot."

"Did he have a record?"

The chief nodded. "Nothing major."

Helma kept her focus on the chief's eyes. His slid
away first. There was more he wasn't telling her; she
was sure of it. She certainly wouldn't have chosen the
name Ernie for the dead man. Every Ernie she'd encoun-
tered had been fastidious, dapper even.

Chief Gallant turned his attention to Officer Lehman,
who returned from the hallway with his gun snapped
back into its holster.

"Find anything, Sid?"

"Everything looks undisturbed to me. You'll have to

check, ma'am, to see what might be missing."

"Point of entry?" Chief Gallant asked.

"Possibly the spare bedroom window." He removed a flashlight from his belt. "I'll check around on the landing outside. Your neighbor might have seen something."

Helma shook her head. "Mrs. Whitney was probably in bed by nine. Wait until morning to ask her, please, and don't frighten her. She's elderly and arthritic."

"This building isn't very well lit," Chief Gallant said, scribbling in his notebook again. "I'll send someone by to talk to your landlord tomorrow."

Helma inspected the rest of her apartment, with Chief Gallant following close behind her. Officer Lehman had left all the doors open and the lights on. She entered the back bedroom first. She only needed to glance around the room to see that nothing had been disturbed.

In her own bedroom, she stood in the doorway, sensing once again that her possessions were out of order. On her bureau, the framed photo of her parents was turned more toward the wall. A corner of the sheet was showing beneath her bedspread. She opened her underwear drawer and was positive someone had lifted her folded underwear and peeped beneath it. She shuddered.

"Has someone been in here?" Chief Gallant asked from the doorway.

"Yes. I can't see that anything's missing. It appears that my belongings have been disturbed."

Helma emptied her underwear drawer on the floor and scooped up her clothes in an armful. "I must wash these things," she said, carrying them to the washing machine in the alcove off the hallway.

Then she stripped the sheets and blankets from her bed while Chief Gallant wrote in his notebook and the washing machine chugged behind them.

"We'll check the counters and doorways for fingerprints, but I seriously doubt we'll find anything." He closed his notebook and slipped it into his pocket. "It could have been kids looking for something to sell. That's a pretty common occurrence."

"I think this is a more deliberate intrusion than that, don't you?" Helma asked, passing him with her armload of bedding. "Excuse me," she said as he stepped back.

She piled the bedding on top of the dryer next to the washing machine and turned back to Chief Gallant.

"First of all," she said, speaking over the spin cycle, ticking off her fingers, "the intruder had to have been watching my apartment to know when I left, unless he was exceedingly lucky. Secondly, he didn't take a thing and I own several valuable objects; the antique vase on the table alone is worth a thousand dollars. He only perused my belongings and hoped I wouldn't be observant enough to notice what he'd done. And thirdly, here you are, following up a routine break-in and not telling me the whole truth about what you know."

Helma Zukas was a keen observer of human behavior. The outer edges of Chief Gallant's eyes tightened and she knew she was right.

"Not all police information is available to the general public, Miss Zukas," he said.

"I'm a public librarian, not the general public, a city employee, the same as you," Helma reminded him. "Besides, you yourself said I was associated with the case."

Chief Gallant folded his hands together and turned them inside out, cracking his knuckles. Helma winced.

Now might be the time to tell him about the yellow slip of paper that had fallen out of the city directory, to show him the incomprehensible list of letters, numbers, and the license plate number. Perhaps they, too, were "associated with the case."

"I appreciate your interest, Miss Zukas," Chief Gallant said in a tone she herself often took with a well-meaning library patron, "but this is a police matter. You're a trained librarian and I'm a trained policeman."

He smiled. "I know I wouldn't be very efficient at *your* job."

"You're patronizing me, Chief Gallant. I hope you don't feel that deductive reasoning skills are restricted to the police."

The chief flushed. "I don't mean . . ." he began.

The washing machine buzzed, announcing the rinse cycle.

"Excuse me," Helma said, turning her back. She poured a capful of thick blue liquid through the open door of the machine, taking her time.

"Now, what's the next step in this investigation?" she asked.

"We'll take a set of your fingerprints so we know whose prints we're picking up off your counters," Chief Gallant told her.

At her kitchen counter, Chief Gallant took Helma's hand in his own and rolled her thumb in the ink pad and then onto a paper with a square designating each finger. His hands were warm and surprisingly larger than her own. She liked the way her skin was so much paler than . . .

Helma cleared her throat. "Do you have any more information about how the murderer got into the library?" she asked, looking with distaste at her blackened fingertips.

"We still believe the victim let him in."

He set her pinkie finger into the ink. "We'll be done here in a minute and then you can get some sleep."

"Fingerprints," Helma said in wonder. "I'm having my fingerprints taken."

"That ink will wash off," Chief Gallant assured her.

Helma held up her hand and stared at the dark-stained whorls and loops.

Officer Lehman returned, buckling his flashlight on his belt. "Looks like the perp jimmied the screen on the bedroom window over your landing. Did you leave the window open?"

"Just an inch or two, for air," Helma told him.

"That's all it takes. You might slip a wooden dowel in the window track so it can't be slid all the way open," he suggested.

Helma nodded wearily.

"Do you have a telephone in your bedroom?" Chief Gallant asked.

"Yes."

"Good. If you hear anything suspicious, call us. We'll keep a car patrolling the area the rest of the night. Let us know if you discover anything missing." Chief Gallant paused. "And the same still goes about the murder victim; call us if you remember anything at all."

The police were gone and Helma was back in bed under fresh sheets when she remembered the notepaper she'd copied the letters and numbers onto, along with the license plate number and the Bellehaven telephone numbers. In her half-asleep state she couldn't recall what she'd done with it. She sat up. Then she remembered: she'd turned the paper over and begun a grocery list. Would it have been of any interest to the intruder? She got out of bed and slipped into her robe and slippers.

There on the table, exactly as she'd left it, with a pencil lying across its midsection, was the piece of paper, undisturbed. Anyone looking at it would have been convinced they were seeing only a grocery list. "Window cleaner," it read. "Lettuce, nonfat milk, chocolate chips."

Once more Helma sat down with another piece of notepaper, turned over her grocery list and carefully copied from it the numbers and letters. "SQ VILKE HRC Mar. 10, April 7, 1469 or 1649." When she was finished, she took an envelope from her desk and slipped the new piece of paper inside. In her precise script she addressed the envelope to herself.

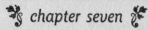

chapter seven

RUTH'S MISSING CAR

On Saturday morning, Helma Zukas awoke with gritty eyes and a pounding head. It was 9:23. She couldn't remember the last time she'd slept in past 8:30. For several long moments she sat groggily on the edge of her bed, breathing deeply and rhythmically, trying to clear her mind of the sensation she was trapped inside a wet cardboard box.

She stayed in the shower until her still darkly smudged fingertips wrinkled. Her legs had a light stubble; she'd shave them later. She resolved to buy herself a new shower curtain, one of the see-through kind. She couldn't clear her mind of Anthony Perkins in *Psycho*.

Helma didn't think the intruder had been inside her closet. Nothing was out of order or alignment. She pulled out a loose, brown skirt and a checkered cotton blouse.

Her apartment had been violated. It had a "bruised" feeling about it, an unpleasant odor that wasn't really there if you tried to sniff it out. Helma lit candles on the table, the counters, in her living room and by the bathroom sink, burning them until the air was fragrant with vanilla, rose, and bayberry.

90

She fixed herself a buttered and jammed English muffin for breakfast, barely tasting it, thinking about the night before, beginning with the calls she'd made from the numbers she'd copied.

The phone call she'd received, the silent one: just before she hung up, she'd heard something, like a click or a tap. She stretched across the table for the slip of paper.

There it was: 676-1649, answer without acknowledgment.

That was the number with the metallic-sounding click. Was that what she'd heard at the end of the silent phone call?

She turned the jam jar back and forth between her palms. It was curious, that metallic click.

Helma picked up the phone and dialed the public library. She recognized Curt's voice. He answered, "Library."

"The correct response is 'Bellehaven Public Library. May I help you?' Now connect me to the reference desk, please," Helma told him.

"Yes, ma'am. Sorry, ma'am."

"Reference. How may I be of assistance?"

It was Patrice. Helma silently groaned, picturing Patrice at the reference desk in her ramrod posture, her darting, suspicious eyes.

"Hello, Patrice. This is Helma Zukas. Would you mind looking in the reverse phone listings of the city directory for a telephone number?"

"Of course not, Helma. That's what we're here for," she said, "to serve the public."

"Thank you. It's 676-1649."

"One moment please."

The phone clicked onto hold. While she waited, Helma watched a group of sailboats racing toward the buoy, their brightly colored jibs stretched taut, splashes of color in the dull day. Helma had once dreamed of owning a sailboat, long ago, before Bellehaven.

"Helma? There's no listing for that telephone number."

"Are you certain?"

Silence. Helma pictured Patrice's back stiffening to imperious planes.

"Certainly I'm certain. Is there a name I can look up for you instead?"

"It must be a new listing," Helma said hastily. "Thank you, Patrice."

The doorbell rang. Corey Marble, the manager's nephew, stood on the doormat, swinging a bucket and a squeegee, a wide grin on his face. A pair of headphones circled his neck like a collar, attached to a Walkman hanging on his belt.

"Morning, Miss Zukas," he said. "I came to do the windows."

Helma frowned at the teenager. "Windows?"

"Yeah, sorry I'm late. I was gaming."

"That's right," she said. She'd forgotten hiring Corey over a week ago. "The outside windows. I have to leave soon so you may as well start on the balcony and finish up out here on the landing."

"Sure thing. Great day, huh?"

Corey stepped past Helma into the kitchen, banging the bucket against the doorjamb. "Is it OK if I leave this stuff here for now?"

He shrugged a bulging backpack off his shoulders and dropped it on the floor by Helma's sink. The hilt of a sword emerged from the top compartment.

"Have you taken to carrying weapons, Corey?" Helma asked. The sword certainly looked real, with a leather-wrapped grip and a tooled scabbard.

"Nah," Corey said. "I had a game this morning and I was the GM."

"The GM?"

"Yeah, the Game Master. I ran the game."

"You fought with swords?"

"That was part of my costume," Corey explained patiently. "It's all mind stuff. You know, like Dungeons and Dragons."

"And you dress up to play? Aren't you a little old for that?"

Corey grinned and nudged his backpack with the toe of his fashionably tattered sneaker. "Everybody does it. There's even some old guys in their thirties; they really get into it. It's fun. You oughta see some of the costumes people make for their characters, Miss Zukas."

"Limited only by their imaginations, you're saying?"

Corey bobbed his head, his enthusiasm waxing. "Anything you can dream up: monsters and princesses, elves, Weeuns, bums, animals, myths. Next time I'm . . ."

"I believe you," Helma said. "Now can you descend to the old mundane world of dirty windows?"

"Sure thing."

He pulled his earphones up over his ears and switched on his Walkman. Helma heard the escaping bass of whatever he was listening to, even over the splashing of the hot water he ran into his bucket.

Gaming. Overgrown boys dressing up and playing mind games. Wasn't life itself game enough?

Helma watched Corey attack her windows with flying soap and water for a few moments and then decided it might be better if she didn't. She cleared away her breakfast dishes, thinking of the metallic click when she'd called the 676-1649 number and the sound on the silent call. Perhaps it was a click on her telephone line, some problem with the wires.

She filled the sink with hot water and washed her dishes. There was a dishwasher in Helma's apartment, which she'd used once in fourteen years. Its clunking mechanisms were too loud an intrusion and she didn't like the strange, sticky yet slick way the dishes felt when they came out of the machine. She stored her extra pots in the dishwasher and washed all her dishes by hand in Ivory dish soap, even when she had company.

By the time she let the still-soapy water out of the sink she'd decided to call 676-1649 again. Helma pulled off her yellow gloves and pushed the telephone buttons. On her balcony, Corey's head and the squeegee—in fact, his whole body—bobbed in time with his music.

"Yes?" the man's voice answered. Helma recognized it as the same voice she'd heard the first time she called.

Helma didn't respond. She waited, covering the mouthpiece with her hand. There was an equal silence on the other end of the telephone.

It came. The metallic click. She concentrated, trying to identify the sound. Metal against metal. Controlled. There was a whisper after the click, like a second part of the sound, but it was so faint that when Helma listened for it, she wasn't sure it was actually there.

Helma hung up her telephone and pushed the redial button.

"Yes?" the man's voice answered in the same intonation. Either it was a recording or the man had an uncanny ability to duplicate his voice exactly each time he answered the phone. Helma waited again and once more she heard the metallic click, but nothing else.

She sat at her table fingering the notepaper. Now might be the proper time to notify Chief Gallant. There was something mysterious—almost sinister— about the soft voice and the strange click. She rolled and unrolled the edge of the paper. Would the chief just take her information and tell her to go back to her library books? Let the "trained policemen" take credit for what the librarian figured out?

Helma's phone rang. After the third ring she picked up the receiver. She didn't say anything, knowing somehow what the call was going to be.

There was silence. Then, elusively, mysteriously, came the metallic click. There was no mistaking it. It was identical to the click in the background of the call she'd just made.

Helma pressed the button on the cradle and dialed Ruth's number. Ruth's phone rang eight times.

"Oh God," Ruth answered, her voice muffled as if she'd taken the receiver under the covers with her.

"Ruth, this is Helma."

"Who else would let the phone ring thirty times?"

"It was only eight, Ruth. You're exaggerating. I'm coming over in a few minutes. There's something I want you to take care of for me."

"Helma. You know how my house upsets you. Why don't you wait and meet me somewhere? Or I can come to your apartment in a couple of hours."

"No. I have errands to run. I'll be there in ten minutes."

"You asked for it," Ruth grumbled and hung up.

Mrs. Whitney was sweeping the landing in front of her door when Helma left her apartment. She wore an old Bellehaven High School varsity sweater over her flowered dress and apron.

"I think it's going to clear up," Mrs. Whitney said. "Better get out and enjoy it."

"You're right," Helma told her. "How did you sleep last night, Mrs. Whitney?"

"How kind of you to ask. I slept like a baby on a log."

"The city noises never wake you up?"

"I'm too old to let noises bother me," she said. She looked wistfully at Corey washing Helma's windows. "That boy's doing a good job."

"I'm glad you reminded me," Helma said. "I forgot to pay him."

The back bedroom screen leaned against Helma's apartment wall and Corey busily soaped the window, his shoulders bouncing, one foot tapping. Helma tapped his arm and he turned off his music.

"What's up?" he asked.

Helma handed him a ten-dollar bill. "When you're finished with these," she said, "will you wash Mrs. Whitney's windows? Tell her your uncle's having you wash everyone's or something."

"Sure thing." Corey told her, grinning and pocketing the money.

"And make sure the screen's secure when you're done with this window," she reminded him.

The streets on the Slope angled steeply away from the bay. Here and there, newer cedar-sided homes with still raw landscaping and broad decks sat incongruously among the multicolored Victorian homes, with their established lawns and gardens and huge, elegant old trees whose roots gently nudged up the sidewalks and shaded deep lawns. Helma frequently took walks on the Slope, especially down the alleys where she could catch glimpses of more private, backyard lives.

Helma chided herself for the unreasonable number of times she checked her rearview mirror. No one was following her. Absolutely not.

Ruth sat at her kitchen table, drinking coffee from a thick white ceramic mug, pausing every now and then to push back her dark hair, which was bushed and tangled around her face. Deep circles and smudged mascara bagged under her eyes. Ruth wore a plaid man's robe with piped lapels, and, obviously, nothing underneath it. One large bare foot rested on the seat of the chair across the table from where she sat.

Helma lifted two art magazines and an unopened letter from the chair catty-corner from Ruth and set them on top of another pile of magazines and newspapers on the table. The room was worse in daylight than Helma had realized the night before.

Dirty dishes, a half-full whiskey bottle, and two empty wine bottles sat on the counter amid a jumble of more papers and mail. A paintbrush soaked in a coffee cup. A jar of marinated artichoke hearts sat with its lid off. There was an ashtray on the table with cigarette butts squeezed in half. Ruth didn't smoke, but Helma knew Ruth had friends who had all manner of habits Helma didn't care to explore.

"Coffee?" Ruth asked, making no move, knowing Helma would refuse, asking only out of politeness.

Helma shook her head. Ruth took another gulp from her cup, her eyes squinting in hangover agony.

Helma opened her purse and removed the envelope addressed to herself and set it on a clear spot on the table.

"I want you to keep this for me. Put it somewhere where you can't lose it." Helma stopped herself from adding, "Where you can find it again."

"I can think of safer places," Ruth said. "Give it to your mother, why don't you?"

"Please, Ruth."

Ruth waved her coffee mug. "OK. I'll put it in my jewelry box. So if I forget, you remember that's where it is, all right?"

"In your jewelry box," Helma repeated.

Ruth rubbed her temples. "I haven't been this hung over in years," she said. "I didn't realize I was drinking so much. In fact, I thought I was showing unusual restraint. He had a bottle of Laphroaig—I always was a pushover for good whiskey. I feel like death. I'll bet I look forty years old this morning, don't I?"

Helma thought Ruth looked closer to fifty. "You look like you had a night out," she said tactfully.

Ruth barked a short laugh. "What a night. To get mixed up with a jerk who stole my boot. Thanks for coming down to pick me up last night . . . this morning, I guess."

"You're fortunate to have only lost a boot . . ." Helma began.

Ruth held up her hand. "No lectures, please. I *know* when I've been stupid."

"How was your lunch with the young artist?"

Ruth frowned as if she were trying to remember. "It was what I expected. I had to pay his way. The little twirp ordered the most expensive dishes on the menu, wouldn't you know. I'm such a sucker for adulation. I had to bring him home and take him to bed to get my money's worth."

Helma stood up and pulled her purse strap over her shoulder.

"Don't worry, Helm. It was safe sex."

"I have to be going now, Ruth. Thank you for keeping that envelope."

"What's your hurry?"

"I want to stop at the library and pick up the specifications for the new reference shelves. I'd like to turn the order in to Mr. Upman on Monday."

"Can't you forget about that place for the weekend? Old Uppie can wait until Tuesday."

"*I'd* like to have the shelving as soon as possible."

Ruth clumsily pulled herself from her chair, distractedly scratching her right breast. "Ah, shelving. How to warm the cockles of a librarian's . . ." Ruth paused, tipping her head as if she heard distant voices.

"Helm, I just remembered something. It's fuzzy because I was definitely not clearheaded, but that guy last night? Well, he asked about you." Ruth shook her head. "Isn't that funny? He said he was new in town, but then he asked about you."

"By name?"

"How else could he ask about you?"

"By appearance. What did he want to know?"

Ruth swayed unsteadily and frowned over Helma's head. "No, it was definitely by name, although he *did* mention your lovely long eyelashes and vibrant locks, so I guess he knew who you were. God, I wish I could remember exactly. Maybe it'll come back later. But now when I think about it, I have this feeling he thought I was drunker than I was. He started with a few jokes about librarians and what they do with library paste, then went on to talk about"— Ruth grinned apologetically at Helma—"their sexual preferences. That's when I think he asked about you. I told him to bugger off, you weren't weird. I remember getting mad, and then he started all that kinky stuff and I made my escape."

Ruth shook her head. "Are you doing anything weird behind my back, Helm? Writing your name on bathroom walls or something?"

"Don't be ridiculous. He was probably one of our difficult patrons."

"I told you he wasn't a local. Weren't you listening? Smooth as butter. Had an answer for everything. Cosmopolitan type, you know?"

"Not really," Helma said.

"No, probably not," Ruth conceded. She fingered an artichoke heart from the open jar and stuffed it into her mouth. "I wonder where he left my car?" she asked while she chewed.

"*Your* car? I thought you said he asked if he could take you home? Why were you in your car?"

"Helmie, Helm dear. 'Taking me home' is a . . . whatchamacallit, you know."

"A euphemism: the substitution of an agreeable term for an offensive one."

"That's right. It didn't start out offensively, though. Wherever he left my car, I hope my boot's still in it. That pair cost me one of my more talented artistic renderings."

"Why don't you call the police," Helma suggested. "Report your car as stolen and give them a description of this man?"

Ruth tapped her front teeth with a fingernail. Her fingernails weren't really dirty; they were stained from all that paint. But they always *looked* dirty.

"I don't think so. Too much explaining to do. Besides, Chief Gallant's the only one I'd want to talk to, and he's too busy with your messy little library murder. Maybe you could drive me down to Squabbly Harbor and we could see if the guy left my car in one of the other parking lots. If we or the police don't come across it by Monday, I promise to inform them of their civic responsibilities."

Helma readjusted her purse strap on her shoulder so it wouldn't wrinkle her blouse. "He could be out of the state by now," she warned Ruth.

Ruth shook her head with certainty. "Not in my battered but faithful car. He wasn't the vintage Saab type, I can assure you."

"But still . . ."

"Have you ever thought about Chief Gallant's name?" Ruth interrupted.

"No I haven't. What about it?"

"Gallant? Just switch the accent to the first syllable. Like out of a fairy tale. Prince Charming and Prince Gallant. It has a white-knight ring to it, don't you think? With a name like that he was destined to become some kind of a lifesaver: a cop, a doctor, a fireman. I can see him as a kid swearing to defend his mother and apple pie and the American way."

Ruth was beginning to ramble. It was time to leave.

There was a knock on the door behind Helma. She stepped aside to let Ruth answer it. Ruth didn't even have a peephole in her door, or a dead bolt, just one flimsy lock with a key she was always losing. Ruth casually pulled her robe closed and ran a hand through her hair before she opened the door. She squinted into the daylight.

"Oh, how convenient. We were just talking about you people," she said. "Did you find my car?"

Two police officers stood outside the door, caps in hands. One of them was Officer Lehman. The other—his badge read George Hall—was older, gray-haired with a slight paunch. Officer Lehman nodded when he saw Helma. Helma acknowledged him with a brief incline of her head.

"You reported it missing?" Officer Hall asked, glancing down at the notebook in his hand.

"Well, no. Not yet. I was going to though, maybe tomorrow or Monday, if I didn't find it first. You guys are certainly on the ball."

"When did you first notice your car had disappeared?" Officer Lehman asked.

Ruth shrugged and raised her arms. Her robe gaped open. The two officers discreetly kept their eyes on her face.

"It wasn't like it disappeared exactly. I was in it and this obnoxious man who was with me became even more obnoxious, so I jumped out and left him with my car." She put a hand on her hip. "I ran for my life, actually."

The two policemen exchanged glances, their faces neutral.

"Did you feel you were in any danger from him?" Officer Hall asked.

"Not really. He was a pencil neck, but in my condition at that moment, he was too much of a weasel to hang out with a moment longer than necessary." Ruth shook her shoulders in distaste.

"Do you think you could recognize him?" Officer Lehman asked.

Ruth bit her lip. "Well, it was night and I'd been drinking . . ." She shrugged. "Yes, I think I could."

"We'd like you to come with us to make an identification."

Ruth looked down at her bare feet, her robe. She touched her face. "I'd have to get dressed, comb my hair, pee, all those essentials, first."

"We can wait."

"So the weasel was going to keep my car, huh?" Ruth asked eagerly. "I was sure he'd ditch it somewhere and disappear from town without a trace."

The two policemen exchanged glances again. Helma was sure she saw Officer Hall give a slight nod to Officer Lehman.

"He was still in your car," Officer Lehman said. The way he said it, cool and matter-of-fact, made Helma's throat tighten.

"How'd you catch him?" Ruth asked. "Was he speeding? Did he freak at the sight of a police car and race off into the night trying to outrun you? He should've known my dear old jalopy couldn't outrun a cop car."

"We found your car parked in the cannery parking lot," Officer Lehman said gently. "He was in the trunk."

"The trunk?" Ruth questioned. "What was he doing in . . ." Her eyes widened. "Oh," she said, covering her mouth.

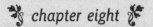

❧ chapter eight ❧

A VISIT WITH
THE POLICE

"**D**on't you dare leave me," Ruth told Helma.

Turning back to the two police officers, she beckoned with a hooked finger and said, "Come in here and wait. You can have a cup of coffee or a glass of whiskey or something."

"Thank you, ma'am," Officer Lehman said, "but we'll wait outside until you're ready."

Ruth shrugged. "Suit yourselves. It won't make me move any faster, if that's what you're thinking."

As the two policemen backed out the open doorway, Ruth put her hand on Officer Hall's arm. "Listen," she said, "I'm not going with you unless my friend Wilhelmina Zukas comes with me. I won't look at a dead body without her."

"That's not a problem, Miss Winthrop. Miss Zukas can accompany you."

"All right, then," Ruth said as if she'd won a point, and slammed the door.

"Ruth," Helma said, moving back to the door. "I'm really not interested in seeing another corpse. The first one was enough."

"Of course you are," Ruth said, pulling Helma's

purse off her shoulder and setting it on the table. "Remember, this guy had a prurient interest in you. Don't you want to see what he looks like? Maybe you'll recognize him."

"If he's dead, it doesn't really matter."

Ruth's face slipped from animated to haggard. "I don't think I can go alone. God, Helm. He was in the trunk of my car." She hugged herself and shivered. "I'll never be able to drive my car again. Every time I opened the trunk I'd see him there, curled around my spare tire. In *my* trunk. Please, Helma."

Helma slid her hand across Ruth's table toward her purse.

"We're friends, Helma, right? We've been friends forever. Who knows, maybe we *will* be friends forever. Two little old lady ghosts gossiping in some gruesome cemetery. You don't really want to miss out on this, do you? Please."

Helma took her hand from her purse and waved toward Ruth's bathroom. "Go get dressed," she said. "I'll go with you."

Ruth smiled gratefully, her big even teeth showing to her gums. "I'll only be a second," she said and strode out of the kitchen, dropping her robe on the floor as she went.

Helma sighed and picked up the robe, listening to Ruth humming in the bathroom. She draped the robe over the back of Ruth's chair and sat down to wait. Ruth was right. Helma *was* curious about the identity of the man who'd asked about her. Being in the public eye at the library left the librarians open to the conjectures of unbalanced citizens. But another body. Another murder in Bellehaven.

"Do you think they found my boot?" Ruth called from her bathroom.

Helma jumped guiltily and saw that without being conscious of it, she'd divided the pile of magazines and letters on the table in front of her by size and patted them into three neat stacks. She folded her hands tightly together in her lap. Helma Zukas was not in the habit of shouting between rooms so she didn't answer Ruth.

Ruth went back to humming a tune Helma thought might be an old Beatles song. The only Beatles music she'd ever been able to recognize was "I Want to Hold Your Hand." Every other song Helma heard by that group had just sounded like another variation of "I Want to Hold Your Hand."

Drawers banged; water ran. Two murders in Belle-haven in barely three days. The last murder Helma remembered was almost a year ago. That had been a classic case of a distraught wife stabbing her philandering husband with a kitchen knife. She wondered idly if kitchen utensils were used in as many domestic crimes as guns. She'd have to look it up.

"Let's go," Ruth said, entering the kitchen.

"Oh, Ruth. What is that outfit?" Helma asked.

"These, my dear, are my corpse-viewing clothes. This is not a time for gaiety."

Ruth wore black, from a black scarf around her head turban-style, to a black sweater and an overlong black skirt, black stockings, and vampish, open-toed black high heels. She towered over Helma. The Avenging Angel, the Grim Reaper, Darth Vader.

"It's a little excessive, I think."

"Then you shouldn't feel compelled to dress like-wise," Ruth said and swept past Helma to throw open the door.

"Oooh," she winced as she stepped into the daylight, raising a hand to her eyes.

The two policemen stood beneath the big willow that was buckling Ruth's sidewalk. Officer Lehman stubbed out a cigarette on the concrete.

"We're ready, gentlemen," Ruth said to the two officers, putting a hand through each of their arms. The policemen didn't skip a beat, Helma had to give them credit for that. They walked on either side of Ruth, both of them shorter than she was.

Helma followed them to the black-and-white police cruiser parked behind her Buick.

Ruth and Helma sat in the backseat, a mesh panel separating them from the two officers in front. The car smelled antiseptically clean, as if it had been scrubbed with a pine-scented detergent.

"Just riding in this car makes me feel guilty," Ruth whispered to Helma. "Like I robbed a 7-Eleven or something."

"Think of it as a taxi," Helma told her.

"My imagination's not that powerful. What do you think happened to this guy we're going to look at? How did he get into my car's trunk?"

"Probably not by himself." Helma tapped on the panel in front of her. "Excuse me," she said. "Please tell us how the man died."

"He was shot," Officer Hall said.

"In my trunk?" Ruth asked.

"No," Officer Lehman said, leaning his head back. "He appears to have been shot somewhere else and then put into the trunk of your car."

"Was it, uh, messy?" Ruth asked. She twisted her hands together, then smoothed her black skirt over her knees.

"There were some newspapers in the trunk," Officer Hall said. "They absorbed whatever might have damaged the trunk's interior."

"Thank God I forgot to take them to the recycler's," Ruth said.

"Do you know who he was?" Helma asked.

"No identification."

"Similar to the murdered man in the library, isn't it?" Helma asked.

Neither officer responded. They rode the rest of the way in silence. Ruth chewed on a thumbnail and kept her face turned toward the window.

Bay Hospital, the smaller and less desirable of the two hospitals in the county, was situated across the street from the police station, a block from the public library. Helma held her hand to her face as they passed the library, just in case one of her patrons should glance in and recognize her.

Officer Hall parked the cruiser in a POLICE CARS ONLY slot and they entered the hospital through the emergency room.

The ten or twelve people in the lobby, plus the desk receptionist, all swiveled their heads toward them. It was Ruth who caught their attention. Her black outfit when everyone else was in short sleeves; her height; her sauntering yet sensual walk; her open, curious face.

"Amazon of the Jungle," a male voice sneered from the chairs lining the wall.

"Pee Wee of the Essentials," Ruth said airily without turning.

The lobby was bare-walled and tile-floored. Sounds echoed back and forth and top to bottom. The clacking of typewriters, voices in various stages of emotional upset and professional calm. A sick child, her eyes listless, her face flushed with fever, leaned against her mother. A man sat calmly holding a bloody towel to his knee.

"We'll take the service elevator," Officer Lehman said, leading them down the hallway.

Helma had a dislike of elevators—she wouldn't quite go so far as to say fear—but a genuine discomfort for the way one was shut inside a space the size of a closet and randomly moved up and down: no doorknobs, no windows, no way out, just faith that some distant mechanism was hauling the box properly between floors and would really disembowel itself because a button the size of a bottle cap had been pushed.

"Can't we take the stairs?" she asked.

"Don't be a goose," Ruth said, taking her arm. "Why on earth walk when you can ride?"

"AUTHORIZED PERSONNEL USE ONLY" read a sign on the elevator door, printed on a square background of fluorescent paint.

"High visibility yellow," Helma observed as Officer Lehman pushed the button beside the door.

"What are you talking about, Helm? You've begun to gibber."

"The background paint on that elevator sign," Helma explained. "It's called high-visibility yellow. It was developed specifically for emergency vehicles and urgent signs. It's not a color that occurs normally in nature, the theory being that it would be more readily recognizable to the public. Unfortunately, people are too inured to red's meaning emergency and don't respond to high-visibility yellow."

"Except to get a headache," Ruth said. "Red makes you think of blood. Sets off all the age-old alarms."

The elevator doors opened to a wide, empty car. Quilted mats hung on the walls. They stepped inside and Officer Hall pushed the number 3 button.

"Aren't we going down to the morgue?" Helma asked.

"Morgue's on three," Officer Hall told her.

"That seems inefficient. It would cost less to keep the basement cool than the third floor." The doors closed like the eye of a lizard. Just the four of them inside a padded box.

"Explain that to the powers-that-be," Officer Hall said from the corner of his mouth.

"Efficiency and economy should be the main concerns of every agency, particularly those operating with funds provided by the taxpayers," Miss Zukas explained.

The elevator hurtled them upward. Helma clasped her hands together to keep from bracing against the walls.

"Well, yeah. You and I agree on that one," he said.

Officer Lehman tucked in his blue shirt more securely. "Did you discover anything missing from your apartment?"

Helma shook her head. How could it take so long to go up two floors? "No. Nothing. Just the general disarray of the rooms."

Ruth squawked and stood away from the hanging mat she'd been slouching against. "Missing? What are you talking about? Your apartment, Helmie? Did someone break into your apartment? Why didn't you tell me?"

The number 3 above the door lit up as the elevator finally dinged to a stop and the doors slid open. Helma dabbed at a thin line of perspiration above her lip.

"It was a minor break-in," Helma told Ruth. "I'll explain it later."

"You'd better."

On the wall in front of them a sign read MORGUE. Under it, a painted hand pointed its index finger to the left. Ruth's chest rose as she took a deep breath. "Do I have to do this?" she asked, her voice gone small.

"It would be a help to us," Officer Hall said. "It'll be brief, I promise."

"Where was he . . . I mean, did he get shot in the face? Is he disfigured?"

"You won't see a thing."

"Says you," Ruth told him.

A dark-haired, youngish man in a lab coat sat at a wooden desk inside the morgue office, filling out forms with a stubby pencil.

"We'd like to see the John Doe brought in this morning," Officer Hall told him.

The attendant set down his pencil and nodded. "Our only guest at the moment. Follow me."

The room they entered was cool but not exceptionally so. Helma sniffed at the chemical odor and breathed more shallowly. She'd expected to see a wall of silvery drawers holding corpses, as on TV, but there was only one sheet-covered shape on a gurney in the middle of the room. Three empty gurneys were lined against one white wall. Another wall was taken up by counters and cupboards and two sinks. She wondered briefly what had happened to Ernie Larsen's body. Was there a grieving family somewhere awaiting his belated arrival?

Ruth grabbed Helma's hand. Her fingers were cold, like metal.

"Are you ready, Miss Winthrop?" Officer Hall asked.

They stood on either side of the gurney that held the sheet-draped outline of a body: Helma and Ruth on one side; the two policemen on the other. The attendant stood at the head, a clipboard in one hand and the other resting lightly on the sheet above the corpse.

Ruth looked up at the ceiling and squeezed Helma's hand. "I swear," she whispered. "I swear I will be more careful, from this moment forward, from now on, forever."

"Amen," Helma added, wiggling the fingers Ruth held to keep her blood circulating.

Officer Lehman nodded to the attendant. In a smooth, tender movement, the attendant pulled back the sheet from the corpse's head, draping it so the body was exposed like a classical bust, bare from just below the shoulders to the top of his head.

There was no blood. His skin was pale enough that the blood might already have been drained from his body. Sunlight from a high window picked out light bristles of facial hair. He looked waxy. Not a very large man, or maybe shrunken by death. Middle-aged, graying at the temples, sharp-nosed, narrow-lipped.

"That's him," Ruth said after one quick look, raising her eyes to a point on the wall behind the officers. "He stole my boot, the little twit. If he could do that to a total stranger, who knows what other underhanded tricks he was up to?"

"Do you know his name?" Officer Lehman asked.

Ruth shook her head. "He told me, but I forgot. It was only his first name, anyway. Something common, like John or Tom."

"How long were you with him?"

"Maybe an hour or two. I met him at Spat's and we had a couple of drinks. Then he asked if he could take me home."

"In your own car?"

"It was easiest," Ruth said so vaguely the police let it pass. "Can't we get out of here now?"

"Then what happened?"

"We parked by the Coast Guard station for a while. He had a bottle of Laphroaig in his car and we brought it with us. We drank a little of that and talked. Then he got kinky and I jumped out and called Helma to come pick me up. That was the last I saw of him."

"What time did you pick up Miss Winthrop?" Officer Hall asked Helma.

"Ruth phoned me at 1:47 A.M. and I picked her up near the pay phones at the Squabbly Harbor Center at 2:10 to 2:12."

Ruth squeezed her hand again and said, "Helma is always accurate in her observations. If she says 2:10 to 2:12, you can bet your last can of black shoe polish that's exactly what time it was."

Helma briskly cleared her throat.

"We're not doubting your word, ma'am," Offi Lehman hastily reassured her.

"You have no reason to doubt my word," Hel said. "I'd only like to say that I've seen this n before. He came into the library yesterday after asking about the college directories. I saw him again at lunch at Saul's Deli. He started to ent then left."

All three looked at Helma. The attendant leaned against the wall doodling on his clipboard, ignoring their conversation.

"Did you speak to him?"

"Only to show him where the college directories were."

"He didn't give any indication of where he was from or what his business might be?"

Helma examined the waxy still features. Ruth had called him a weasel, a twit. Now he was nothing. He looked like a sculptor's blank of a human, a mannequin devoid of personality, without life, no past or future. She cleared her throat again.

"You might try searching in the vicinity of the harbor for a dark blue or black rental car with the license plate HRZ 417," Helma told them.

"A rental car?" questioned Officer Hall.

"What was that license plate number?" Officer Lehman asked, scribbling in his notebook.

"HRZ 417. I believe we've seen enough here," Helma said and pulled Ruth away from the gurney.

"Did you find my boot?" Ruth asked over her shoulder.

"We found a cream-colored size eleven woman's boot in the back seat."

"Good. Drop it by my house later today, if you don't mind."

The two policemen followed Ruth and Helma out of morgue.

Miss Zukas, Miss Winthrop. Would you mind g to our office to tell us a little more about association with the deceased?"

hy do you think we should look for a rental car?" Officer Hall.

ou now," Helma told them firmly. "I have to get to fi . . I have errands to run, plus important work me if at the library. Check the parking lots and call u find the car. We'll talk then: HRZ 417."

"You won't be leaving town, will you, Miss Winthrop?" Officer Lehman asked.

"No, why?" She turned back to him, her hands on her hips. "You guys don't think that I . . . ?"

"Just in case we have more questions," Officer Hall quickly answered. "That's all."

Helma led Ruth toward the stairs.

Ruth held back. "No way, Helmie. My legs aren't working well enough to navigate steps. It's the elevator or just leave me here."

Helma swallowed and pushed the button to call the elevator, finally pulling her hand from Ruth's and straightening her collar.

"You've got a lot of explaining to do, you know," Ruth hissed as the elevator doors opened.

"I can relate what I know, but I'm not sure that 'explanations' are required, or possible," Helma told her. She pressed the round button marked LOBBY and longingly watched the door close on Officers Lehman and Hall.

"Why didn't you tell me about the break-in? And how do you know about a rental car?"

The elevator stopped. Were they stuck? The light above the door read 2, only 2. The doors opened and Helma saw three men waiting: two policemen and a prisoner in a green jumpsuit with a plaster cast on his leg. A chain fastened his handcuffs to a wide leather belt around his waist. Each policeman held one of the prisoner's elbows.

Miss Zukas held up her hand.

"Please wait for the next car," she said in her silver-dime voice. "It will be more comfortable for all of us."

One of the policemen opened his mouth but Helma firmly pushed the LOBBY button again, and then again, and said, "Thank you."

"It was a harmless break-in," she told Ruth when the elevator doors closed. "Probably juveniles. As for the rental car, I saw the deceased enter it outside the deli. I thought he might have accidentally picked up a piece of paper I left on the reference desk so I took note of his license number."

"And then you just happened to trace the license number and your apartment just happened to be broken into, and this same character just happened to pick me up at a bar, get me drunk, ask questions about you, steal my boot, and end up stuffed in my trunk?"

"Strange things *do* happen, Ruth."

"Hah!"

They left the elevator, Ruth waving her arms like a tall crow. Helma reached back inside and pushed the 2 button on the elevator panel. The hubbub in the lobby paused as they passed through. Ruth didn't notice. Her voice rose in indignation.

"Too many coincidences, Helm. I'm not sure I believe a word of it."

Ruth stopped in front of the street doors and turned to confront Helma. "Wait a minute. Does this have anything to do with the envelope you gave me?"

Helma looked up into Ruth's brightly made-up face, crowned by her black turban.

"Your voice carries quite effectively, Ruth," she said, pushing open the glass door. "It's best if we continue this conversation outside."

Ruth marched through the door ahead of Helma, adjusting her turban and pulling herself taller, her spine stretching, her shoulders squaring, her chin lifting. Helma was familiar with this "heightening" of Ruth's. Ruth was uncertain; she was warming up to belligerency. Helma had seen Ruth perform the same physical magic since they were children.

"Let's go down by the creek and I'll tell you what little I do know," Helma said.

"All of it?" Ruth demanded. "Everything?"

"Every fact I'm certain of," Helma assured her.

*   *   *

A narrow stream ran through the center of town and past the civic buildings. It twisted a rocky path beneath the streets and through a ravine the city had spent millions reinforcing with concrete. For several blocks, a narrow belt of grass and picnic tables and benches skirted the banks of the creek. At night, the homeless who found the Mission too crowded or too stifling spread their sleeping bags close to the water, packing up and going on their way again by the first light before the Parks Department attendants began their daily rounds. Had the late Ernie Larsen had the chance to spend a calm night sleeping beside the stream?

Ruth and Helma walked behind the courthouse and down the sloping bank to a wooden bench overlooking the water. Ruth sniffed disdainfully as they passed a sculpture of a stylized eagle brooding over the creek. It had been the winner of a countywide competition. Ruth's entry of a decidedly phallic mountain had been passed over by the judges. "Provincial conservative yahoos," Ruth had called them.

Ruth dropped on the bench and stretched out her legs. She patted the seat beside her.

"Sit down. Tell all."

Helma placed her purse on the bench between them and crossed her legs at her ankles.

"There's actually not much to tell," she began.

"That kind of evasive bullshit doesn't work with me, Helm."

Helma sighed. There was no point in bringing up Ruth's language to her. "It began with the murder in the library," she said.

"That bum? What about him?"

"I'm not sure. He was very intent on using the city directory the day he was murdered."

"No kidding?" Ruth laughed. "How many bums pull into town on the afternoon freight and hightail it to the local library to use their reference collection?"

"That's a very astute observation, Ruth."

"Thank you. So then what?"

"You must realize it's all conjecture on my part and really too farfetched to take to the police."

"Helm!"

"Helma," Helma corrected.

"Just get on with the details."

"A yellow piece of paper fell out of the city directory the morning we opened after the murder. I set it on the reference desk. The man we just saw in the morgue came into the library and dropped—or pretended to drop—a notebook onto the desk. After he retrieved his notebook, the piece of yellow paper had disappeared."

"So you don't know what was on the paper?"

"I copied it. Then I made another copy and put it in the envelope for you to keep."

"What was it? What did it say?"

"Keep your voice down, Ruth, if you would please. The paper held a series of numbers and letters that made no sense whatever."

Ruth nodded her head vigorously. "They must have made sense to somebody. Was that why your apartment was broken into? To see if you had it?"

"If the man in the morgue took the paper from the desk, why would he care if I had another copy? It was just gibberish."

Ruth frowned and leaned on her knees, her chin in her hands. "Maybe someone else thought you had it. Maybe the weasel saw you make your copy and thought it was too dangerous to leave it in your meddling hands."

"I still assume it was juveniles."

"Then they should have stolen something. But they didn't, did they?"

"No. They were actually quite tidy."

Ruth rocked back and forth. "Why did that creep ask

so many questions about you? None of it computes."

"I'm not sure we can force any of it to 'compute,' Ruth."

Ruth sat up and faced Helma. "Do you ever think about dead people, Helma?"

"In light of the past couple days, it's come up. Why?"

"I was just curious. Seeing this guy . . . Dead is *so* dead, isn't it? So . . . I don't know . . . permanent, I guess. And having that dream about my old man kind of stirred up a few ancient thoughts."

"About your father?"

Ruth nodded and looked at the stream rushing over the rocks below them. Two young boys were throwing stones at a beer can jammed between two rocks. *They ought to be home mowing their lawns or cleaning their rooms*, Helma thought.

"He could be a real bastard, you know," Ruth said, her eyes on the boys. "He died before I realized just what a rat he was. Shiftless, spineless, futureless. A real boozer and carouser. If he hadn't died so conveniently in that wreck, I'm sure it wouldn't have been long before my mother kicked him out. In fact, it's probably his fault that her life was so short."

"I remember him, too," Helma said. "I was too young to understand all his adult weaknesses. Sometimes I was jealous of the way he played with you."

"When he was boozed up, you mean. He was either God's most loving father on earth, or the meanest prick who ever took a breath. I never knew what to expect. Poor Mom. It was years before I realized why Aunt Rachel called her a saint."

"Perhaps he'd be contrite if he were alive to consider his past."

"Don't bet on it," Ruth said. "If you want to talk about jealousy, I nearly choked on my own bile when I saw you with your family, all your uncles and aunts and grandparents jabbering away in Lithuanian and drinking and fighting and joking around. It looked perfect from the outside."

"They *were* demonstrative," Helma conceded.

"I never could figure out why you turned out the way you did."

"To what are you referring?" Helma asked.

Ruth flushed. She stuck the nail of her paint-stained index finger between her front teeth.

"I don't know. Undemonstrative, I guess. Why don't we go look at that piece of paper with the code on it?"

"Ruth, you're jumping to conclusions. It's a simple piece of paper with a patron's doodlings on it. That doesn't mean it's a 'code.' "

"Well, you must think it's pretty important or you wouldn't have asked me to hide a copy for you."

"Not hide, keep."

"Oh, Helm. Stop dancing around the bare truth. Let's go."

Ruth stood. Helma remained seated. "We can look at it later. I think I'll walk over to the library and do that shelving order."

"Are you sure?"

"I'm certain."

Ruth patted her turban. "I'll have to get one of those big, brave policemen to give me a ride home."

"Maybe he'll let you play with his siren," Helma said.

"Helm! I can't believe you said that." Ruth laughed with her head thrown back and her mouth wide. "See, you can't always keep your sense of humor locked up as tight as your . . ." She stopped. "Well, then. I'll talk to you later."

"Good-bye, Ruth."

"Bye. Thanks for viewing the weasel's remains with me." She shuddered. "I hope that's the last time we have that pleasure."

After Ruth left, Helma watched the creek babble

and burble past. The water was high from spring snow melting in the mountains. In two months it would drop to a thin stream that curved through the deepest slice of the creekbed, leaving the now-submerged rocks high and dry. Then, the children who now threw rocks into the stream could easily cross the creekbed, jumping from rock to rock over the tamed water.

Helma spent a few minutes thinking of the dead, too, remembering what her mother had said about her father's family being a tornado, sucking everyone up.

She remembered their petty quarrels and violent reconciliations and loud, incontestable opinions. And always, surrounding them with all of the magic and sentimentality of an Irish mist, was Lithuania. Her grandfather ached for his homeland. His sons, who had never set eyes on that Baltic nation, felt the Russian takeover as a personal loss, depriving them of their birthright as surely as if they'd been led to the borders of Eden and rudely had the gates slammed in their faces, never to be allowed to enter.

Lithuania beckoned, Helma had believed from their rhapsodizing, like a stirring spiritual and someday, when they could shuck off those clumsy bodies, the chariots would swing low and they'd climb aboard, dressed in their heavenly best, to be deposited on those far sandy shores like lost and loved children returned to their anxiously waiting parents.

Well, she hoped that's where they all were: her grandparents, her father, and his five brothers and sisters.

Finally, Helma stood and slipped her purse back over her shoulder. If she worked uninterrupted in the quiet of the Saturday library, she should be able to finish the shelving order in an hour, two at the most.

The path along the creek would take her to another path just beneath the library. The smell of the water was like fresh leaves and new earth. Helma stopped, closed her eyes, and breathed deeply.

Then she opened her eyes and began walking, her crepe soles firm on the graveled path that led up to the library's sidewalk.

❧ chapter nine ❧

INTERLUDE: LUNCH WITH MR. UPMAN

"**G**ood afternoon, Miss Zukas," Mrs. Carmon, the circulation clerk, said when she saw Helma. She hurriedly bundled up what looked like a ball of baby blue yarn and a crochet hook and slipped it beneath the counter.

The library was unusually quiet for a Saturday afternoon. The regulars were in the magazine/newspaper section and a few patrons worked the card catalog.

"Hello, Mrs. Carmon. A quiet day today?"

"Only momentarily. You should have been here an hour ago. People everywhere and at the same time we kept receiving crank phone calls with no one on the other end. I've only just now been able to catch my breath. Are you on the reference desk today?"

"I have some paperwork I'd like to finish, that's all," Helma told her.

"You're such a dedicated librarian," Mrs. Carmon cooed.

"It's part of being a responsible member of the profession," Miss Zukas informed her. "I see there's a backlog of returned books to be reshelved." She nodded to the carts of books behind the circulation desk.

Mrs. Carmon squared her shoulders. "Patty has a touch of the flu today. The books will all be back on the shelves when the afternoon page comes in."

"I've done my share of reshelving," Helma told her. "It doesn't hurt any of us to reshelve. On the contrary, it sharpens the skills. We exist so the public can have ready access to knowledge and reading pleasure."

"I . . ." Mrs. Carmon began. Helma held up her hand.

"I really have to go to my desk now. Good day."

George Melville sat at the reference desk, his head bent over a sketch pad. Helma glimpsed a surprisingly accurate depiction of the chestnut tree on the library lawn.

"Hello, Mr. Melville," Helma said, stopping beside the desk. "It looks like a slow Saturday."

George Melville raised his head and scratched his beard, squinting at Helma. "When are you going to start calling me by my given name like everyone else, Helma? We've been working together for three years. It's not hard to say: George. Monosyllabic, even."

"It's hardly proper for the public to hear its professionals of the opposite sex using a bantering tone with one another. Are you and Patrice sharing desk duty today?"

George Melville nodded, rolling his eyes upward. "And a jolly time we're having. Patrice said you'd called this morning and asked her to check a phone number in the city directory. You sure tapped the jugular vein of her curiosity. What are you doing here when you could be out frolicking?"

"I wanted to finish the new shelving order. It's easier to concentrate when it's quiet."

"Today's the day, I guess. The boss is gracing us with his presence, too."

"Mr. Upman?" Of all the library staff, Mr. Upman and Patrice were the two people she'd most prefer to avoid.

"None other. He's wrapped up in the budget. Good idea, I think, keep him out of our hair."

"Oh, Helma," Patrice said, stepping up behind George Melville. Her glasses hung on their gold chain, tangling with the beaded necklace around her neck. "We certainly could have used your experience a little while ago, couldn't we, George?"

Helma didn't trust any words from Patrice that smacked of praise. George Melville frowned. "How's that?" he asked Patrice.

"Well," Patrice said, talking to Helma, not George Melville. "A most interesting reference question. A man, he might have been a distinguished anthropologist, a research professor probably, is doing a study on the indigenous diets of various ethnic groups. You would have found it fascinating. He believes that if members of every group ate only their historical diet—if the Japanese ate rice and the Eskimos ate whales or whatever—and didn't cross over into the food of other cultures, the human race would be virtually free of disease."

"And how does that involve Helma?"

Helma was grateful George Melville asked it, so she didn't have to.

"Oh, I'm sure Helma could have given him tips on what her ethnic group ate. I wasn't much help, of course, because my roots are Anglo-Saxon and our diet has always been varied, not limited by what can be foraged in the forests and jungles."

George Melville flipped to a clean page in his sketch pad and furiously scribbled. He held it out of Patrice's range but so Helma could read it: HE WAS A NUT CASE—P'S SOUL MATE.

"I recall my grandfather mentioning a particularly meaty beetle," Helma said. "I'll be happy to ask my aunt if you like."

Patrice grimaced and George Melville closed one eye in a wink.

"Excuse me," Helma said. "I have work to do."

"Did you discover the identity of the mysterious man?" Patrice called after her.

Helma stopped midstride and turned to face Patrice. "I beg your pardon?"

"The man at that telephone number. I thought when I couldn't find his number in the city directory that of course you must have quoted me an incorrect telephone number, so I dialed it just to ascertain that it was an actual number."

Helma could think of nothing to say to Patrice's effrontery. She waited to hear the rest.

Patrice shook her head, her nostrils flaring slightly. "All he would say was 'Yes?' even though I asked him for his name and address. Do you have business, or personal dealings with him?"

George Melville lowered his head and covered his eyes with his hands.

"I believe, Patrice," Helma said, "that you have gone beyond your librarian's duties and passed into the realm of invasion of privacy."

Patrice pursed her lips. "I was only trying to help, Helma. Isn't that why you phoned the library, for assistance?"

"You rendered all the assistance I required when I called. In the future, please confine your excessive curiosity to your own personal business," Helma said and left. Behind her she heard Patrice's indignant voice, catching the word, "ungrateful."

The door to Mr. Upman's office stood open. He sat at his desk in front of a sheaf of papers. She swallowed once and tried to pass his office soundlessly, admitting to herself that yes, tip-toeing was exactly what she was doing.

"Miss Zukas!" Mr. Upman called.

Helma stopped, caught. "Good afternoon, Mr. Upman."

He beckoned her into his office. Helma took one

step inside the door, trying to appear in a hurry, as though this was an unavoidable pause on an important mission.

"I heard there was another murder in town last night." He rubbed both hands across his bald head, front to back. "What's going on in Bellehaven? I moved here thinking I was leaving crime behind. This is a city—a town actually, a small town—with one of the lowest crime rates in the country. Do you know I lost my wallet in K Mart once; some fourteen-year-old boy found it and turned it in. Nothing missing. Not so much as a dollar bill. Nothing. And in K Mart! I don't even lock my house half the time. And now this. Not that it's any comparison, but last night some punks rifled through my car."

"Did they take anything?"

"Not that I could tell. They dumped the contents from the glove compartment on the floor and pulled the seat covers off the seats. I won't leave my car unlocked again, that's for sure."

"Did you call the police?"

Mr. Upman nodded. "This morning. That's when I found out about the second murder. The police force must be busy investigating it because the chief of police himself came out to check on my petty problem."

"What did he say?"

"He thought it was probably juvenile delinquents. No supervision. They're under the effects of television and all those violent rock music videos." Mr. Upman thumped his finger on his desk. "It's a combination of modern technology and the insane urge of Americans to leapfrog ahead of one another that causes the degradation of our values. Consume, consume. That's all anyone thinks about. There's no sense of family or morality. Life is fragmented, and children today are irresponsible."

Helma remembered reading a similar complaint, attributed to Socrates. " 'They have bad manners, contempt for authority; they show disrespect for elders and love chatter in place of exercise,' " she quoted from memory.

"You're exactly right, Miss Zukas." Mr. Upman glumly stared down at his desk. "And now another murder."

"I'd say that Bellehaven's paid its dues for the year," Helma said. "It's a sad coincidence that these incidents took place within a few days of one another."

"Maybe, but it certainly feels like a deteriorating situation." Mr. Upman looked up at Helma. "You're not scheduled for the reference desk today, are you?"

"I just came in to put together that shelving order for the medical reference section," Helma told him, turning toward the door.

"Oh. Well, I was going to work on the budget, but I keep getting distracted by our crime wave. First, a body in the library. I heard they found this second man in the trunk of a car."

"I'll go work on that order now," Helma said, taking another step.

"Saturday's no time to be here working, not for either of us. Have you had lunch yet?"

"No, but I'd prefer to get that order out of the way."

"Nonsense. I insist. It's my treat. The shelving order can be done on Monday." He waved his hand toward the papers on his desk. "So can the budget. In fact the budget could be summed up in one word: 'Inadequate.' With the new computer system, we'll have to cut back our serials orders, I'm afraid."

"We could hold off on automation," Helma reminded him.

Mr. Upman shook his head. "If we do, we'll be left behind."

"By whom?"

"Other libraries, the modern world."

Mr. Upman stepped from behind his desk and

before Helma knew what was happening, she found herself being herded from the library through the back entrance. At least it wasn't past the reference desk and George Melville and Mrs. Carmon, or worst of all, Patrice.

"What about Saul's Deli?" Mr. Upman asked as they stepped onto the pavement. "We can walk; it's a pleasant enough day."

"That would be fine."

"I'm always tempted by their pies. Homemade." He patted his midriff. "Their cherry pie is deadly."

Helma laughed politely and stepped around a woman watering plants in front of the Petite Women's Boutique. The planter boxes along the street were already luxuriant with pansies, geraniums, and ferns.

Helma ordered her usual roast beef on white with just a little butter and a glass of iced tea.

"Is that all?" Mr. Upman asked when the order was set on their table. "No chips, salad, soup?"

"No, thank you."

"You're a cheap date," he said, arranging his own triple-decker club sandwich and soup and chips in front of him.

"I'm neither a date nor cheap," Helma informed him.

Mr. Upman ducked his head. "I was only trying to make a joke. I meant no offense."

"I accept your apology," Helma allowed and cut her sandwich into quarters.

"Do you eat out often?" Mr. Upman asked.

"Only when it's convenient. I find my own cooking preferable to most restaurant food."

"I wish I could say the same. After my wife died, I began eating most of my meals out, but they never taste quite right, do you know what I mean?"

"Too many carbohydrates," Helma said.

"Exactly. Starch and grease."

"I wasn't aware you'd been married," Helma said.

Mr. Upman looked above Helma's head. He swallowed a bite of sandwich. "For eighteen years. Cancer."

"I'm sorry."

"It was fast. That was the only blessing. So I didn't actually leave the big city just because of the crime. After Allie died I needed a complete change of scenery. It's been a good move. I shouldn't complain because of a couple of murders and kids fooling around in my car. I've just become used to the idea that Bellehaven is one of the last bastions of peace and sanity."

"I think we have to look upon the last few days as a temporary aberration. The crimes will be solved soon and we'll all be able to return to our normal existences."

"I hope you're right. I know we can't run away from crime. I remember when I was a child and life seemed so safe." Mr. Upman laughed. "That's funny when I think of it because you know where I grew up?"

"No, I don't."

"In Las Vegas. My father was a church pastor. He and my mother considered themselves missionaries to the gambling heathens. I'm sure they saw a lot of life's seamier side, but they kept me protected from it." Mr. Upman raised his Coke in a salute.

"Are they still living?" Helma asked.

"They died in a plane crash." He folded the straw from his Coke like an accordion. "It's ironic. They were on their way to a vacation in Florida. It was their fortieth anniversary and I'd bought them the tickets."

"I'm sorry."

He looked out the window, his myopic eyes gone distant. Then he smiled at Helma and asked, "You're not a Bellehaven native, are you?"

Helma shook her head. He must have read her file at least once over the years. "Michigan," she said. "I came out to Washington after I graduated from library school. I intend to stay."

"And your friend?"

"Whom do you mean, Mr. Upman?"

"Ruth Winthrop. But please call me Al."

Helma thought of trying to call Mr. Upman Al. No, it wouldn't do at all.

"It's difficult to predict whether Ruth will stay in Bellehaven or not."

"She still manages to maintain a rather active private life, I understand," Mr. Upman said, dabbing at his lips with a paper napkin.

Helma pushed the remainder of her sandwich aside. "From what *I* understand, Mr. Upman, you might be a better judge of the level of activity in Ruth's private life than I."

Helma noted with surprising pleasure the flush of red that began at Mr. Upman's collar and traveled up his face over his ears to the glistening top of his head. He coughed into his napkin and fussed with his sandwich.

Helma stood up. "Thank you for lunch, Mr. Upman. I believe I'll heed your suggestion and save the library shelving problems until Monday."

"Wait, Miss Zukas . . . Helma," Mr. Upman pleaded, standing.

Helma paused, then noticed how the couple closest to their table was watching with interest. She gave them her professional smile and they bent back to their food.

Mr. Upman shredded the napkin in his hands. "I'm sorry if I offended you, Miss Zukas. I'm a little rusty at this sort of thing. I'd like to take you to dinner or a movie some evening. I mean, if you'd care to accompany me."

Mr. Upman's eyes were distorted to huge sorrow behind his thick lenses.

"I'm afraid a situation of that nature might interfere

with our professional association," Helma told him.

"But my wife was a librarian," he said.

"I'd like to think about it."

He nodded. "I understand. I'll telephone you after working hours."

"That would be preferable."

Outside the deli, Helma glanced at her watch. If she hurried, she could catch the 1:40 bus. She lengthened her stride and then paused. It was a warm day. She was wearing her sturdy shoes and it was less than two miles to her apartment at the Bayside Arms. It would be far healthier to walk.

Ruth would have said Mr. Upman was "making a pass" at Helma. But she didn't think that was the case. He'd been too . . . wistful. It was odd that she'd never considered before that Mr. Upman had a private life, that he might even be lonely.

Helma strode at a steady pace through town, past the brick museum, the antique stores, the espresso cart in front of the Nordstrom store, coordinating her steps and arm-swinging and breaths, barely glancing at the shoppers. Helma rarely shopped purposelessly and couldn't understand the attraction of wandering from store to store simply looking for items to buy.

There was talk of a mall being built at the edge of town and Helma feared for Bellehaven. She'd read what was happening in other cities: empty storefronts, decreased revenues, and increased crime, the larger shops vacating the city to the smaller shops, which fought for the attention of shoppers who cared more about being able to purchase their hearts' delight all under one climate-controlled roof.

Thinking about the potential decline of Bellehaven, Helma slowed down and purposely took note of the busy street with its Victorian era buildings, the trees that shaded the walks, the bright awnings. She noticed the women with children pulling on their arms, babies in strollers, young couples leaning into each other and meandering along the sidewalks, white-haired women with their hands through each other's arms, even the outlandish group of young people with their faddishly torn clothes and wild hair. Would they all simply transplant themselves to the mall without noticing any difference except that it was easier to park? No sense of loss for the town left behind?

Helma left the city streets behind and followed the sidewalk that curved along the wide boulevard above the scoop of the bay. The slightest midday breeze rippled the bay, stirring the salted air off the water. The tide was in, filling the rocky scallops that made tide pools when it turned.

The afternoon hung gray, not with the threat of rain, but with the undiffused calmness of light that could be morning or afternoon. After fourteen years in Bellehaven, Helma had come to feel most comfortable in this undemanding light, which didn't require sunglasses or promise rain or threaten to fade her carpets or furniture.

Helma was avoiding what was really on her mind: murder. The dead Ernie Larsen, the dead unidentified man who'd approached both her and Ruth, the break-in, the yellow piece of paper. *Murder.* Just the growling sound of the word made her heart pound. Murder had nothing to do with her.

She strode past the Seascape Condominiums, the Baywatch Apartments, more unnamed buildings that pridefully and expensively faced the water. Hot air from cars passing too close blew against her. Helma wished that the city had placed the sidewalk farther from the street.

"Look out!" a voice cried, and the next thing Helma knew she was being tumbled from the sidewalk into the Oregon grape bushes, falling, rolling onto her stomach, sharp leaves prickling through her clothing. Another body was tangled with hers. Helma pushed at it, then used her fists.

"Ouch! Hold on!"

Helma struggled to sit up, straightening her blouse, pulling down her skirt.

She looked into the face of a young man wearing a helmet with neon stripes and a shiny tight black-and-green outfit like the bicyclists wore, except for knee and elbow pads. On his feet were black rollerblades.

"Are you all right?" he asked. A sparse mustache barely covered his upper lip.

"I'm not sure yet."

He jumped up and peered up the boulevard. "That bas . . . idiot. He could have killed you. Did you see him?"

"No. Who? I thought you ran into me."

He shook his head and removed his helmet, shaking a sweaty head of brown hair. "Not me. Some fool in a car. He drove right up on the sidewalk. Must've been drunk."

Helma pulled a twig from her hair. "What kind of car was it?"

"Geez, I don't know. Green, or gray. I didn't pay much attention."

Helma held out her hand. "I'm most grateful to you. You probably saved my life."

He shook her hand, then helped her out of the bushes. "I was just going to say something to you before he came along. You work with Eve, don't you?"

"Eve Oxnard? Yes. Do you know Eve?"

He nodded, his brown eyes deepening soulfully like a young animal's. "Yeah, we're . . . friends."

"You live above the pizza parlor?" Helma asked.

"For now, anyway."

"I see," Helma said.

"Well, if you're okay, I'd better get going." He fastened his helmet beneath his chin.

Helma brushed the back of her skirt. "I have an Aunt Em who was happily married for sixty-two years. I know you're not married but she liked to say that to make a relationship work, each partner couldn't just give fifty percent; each had to give one hundred percent."

"Tell Eve that."

"Now that I've told you I might tell her," Helma said.

He waved and skated away, his arms swaying with every forward stride.

Helma resumed her walk home, close to the inside edge of the sidewalk. A car's engine raced behind her and she spun around, her heart pounding.

Someone drunk, Eve's friend had thought. In the middle of the day? She walked faster, hoping that's all it had been, someone drunk, a stranger.

Helma crossed the Bayside Arms parking lot, picking up a discarded Burger King cup and tossing it in a trash can. She glanced at her empty parking slot and gasped before she remembered her car was at Ruth's. She'd have to retrieve it later. She wasn't up to facing Ruth again so soon.

Helma changed her clothes and fixed a glass of iced tea and was just opening the door to her balcony when her mother called.

"Another murder, Helma! What do you think of that? I just heard it on the radio. They found a man's body stuffed in a car trunk down by the harbor!"

"Hello, Mother," Helma said, absently stirring artificial sweetener into her tea. "Yes, I did hear about it. It appears there aren't many facts available yet."

"The police probably know plenty. We're always the last to know, aren't we? There's a killer loose in this town and they're not telling us enough so we can protect ourselves."

"How was your ceramics class last night, Mother?" Helma asked and took a sip of her iced tea while her mother described the ceramic kissing Dutch boy and girl she was painting. Two white tugboats chugged toward the opening of the bay, probably heading out to meet an incoming freighter. A sea gull wheeled above her balcony, screeching raucously and flapping back toward the water.

Helma's doorbell rang. "Excuse me, Mother. Someone's at the door. Can I call you back?"

"You just go right ahead and answer it. I'll wait. It might be a salesman you can get rid of."

Helma sighed and set the phone down on the counter, pointing the mouthpiece toward the wall.

It was Chief Gallant. He wore casual gray pants and a knit shirt and his hair wasn't as carefully combed as it had been in the library. He grinned when Helma opened the door. Helma tucked a strand of hair behind her ear.

"Am I disturbing you?" he asked.

"No," Helma said uncertainly, glancing down at his navy sneakers.

"I'd like to speak with you for a few minutes, if I may?"

"This is an official visit, I presume?"

"Yes, if you have the time."

Helma wasn't exactly comfortable about discussing official matters with a police chief dressed so casually, but she opened her door.

"Please. Come in. Would you like a glass of iced tea?"

"That sounds fine. Thank you."

Helma picked up the telephone. "Mother," she said. "I have company so I'll call you back later."

"I heard a man's voice?" her mother questioned, breathless.

"Yes, you did."

"Who is it?"

Helma didn't answer.

"Is it Chief Gallant?"

"Yes, Mother. It is."

"Oh, Wilhelmina! That's wonderful! You go and have

a nice time with that dear man. Any woman would feel safe with him, wouldn't she? No matter how many murderers were loose in this town."

"Good-bye, Mother. If I don't talk to you tonight, I'll see you for dinner tomorrow," Helma said and gently replaced the phone on its cradle.

Chief Gallant stood in front of the sliding glass doors to Helma's balcony and watched the two tugs nearly to the mouth of the bay.

"Beautiful view," he said, turning to Helma. "I've lived here my entire adult life and I'm still not used to it."

"It's always different, depending on the weather and light." She poured his iced tea from a pitcher and handed the glass to him. "I don't imagine you came here to chat with me about the view."

"No, you're right. I didn't."

"Let's sit on the balcony," Helma said, leading the way through the glass door.

They sat in Helma's white wicker chairs, facing each other across her glass-topped table. A breeze off the bay rustled the leaves of the potted daisies. Helma folded her hands in front of her tea and waited for Chief Gallant to begin.

"I understand you were able to identify the man in the morgue this morning," he said, speaking as casually as he had about the view.

"Not identify," Helma corrected, "recognize."

"Recognize," Chief Gallant repeated. "Could you tell me what you told the officers?"

"It's very insignificant, actually. The man whose body was in the morgue came into the library to ask about collegiate data. He said that he had a son who was about to attend college. But that means nothing. Hundreds of people pass through the library daily."

Chief Gallant nodded. "I remember: the highest circulation statistics in the state."

"Per capita," Helma amended.

"Officer Lehman said you suggested we check the vicinity for a rental car. You even supplied a license number. Could you explain how that came about?"

"Did you find the car?"

Chief Gallant crossed his legs and leaned back, holding his iced tea on his knee. "You tell me what you know, and I'll tell you what I know. Deal?"

Helma turned her glass so the ice cubes clinked against the sides. "I prefer to call it an agreement. It's probably of no consequence, but on the morning after the murder in the library, a piece of paper fell out of the city directory while a patron was using it. I set the paper on the desk, and after the most recently deceased gentleman was at the reference desk to ask about the college directories, the piece of paper was gone. Then, while I was having lunch with my mother at Saul's Deli, the same man stepped into the deli but then left, presumably because it was crowded. I ran after him. I couldn't catch up with him, but I made a note of his license plate number."

"Do you frequently remember license plate numbers?"

"I'm an observant woman."

"And how did you know he was driving a rental car?" Chief Gallant asked. His eyes narrowed. He watched Helma without blinking.

Helma returned his gaze just as steadily. "I was curious, that's all. His behavior piqued my curiosity so I checked on the license plate number. My sources are not of any consequence."

Chief Gallant continued to gaze at Helma without speaking. Helma recognized this as a police tactic to encourage her to say more. It was an interviewer's trick she'd once read about. People had a natural inclination to fill empty pauses in a conversation, frequently divulging more than they intended. Helma sipped her tea and said nothing. Finally, Chief Gallant leaned forward across the table. Helma started to lean back, away from his big frame and intense eyes. But no, that was giving him the advantage and besides, being closer to Chief Gallant wasn't *that* unpleasant.

"Do you remember what was written on the piece of paper?" he asked.

Helma frowned. She couldn't remember, not exactly. "There were letters and numbers which made no discernible sense. A series of letters and four numbers. I recall a 6 and a 9."

"Nothing else? It might be very important to this case. We *are* trained to make sense out of information other people believe is insignificant."

There it was again, the polite condescension. "Are you referring to the untrained populace—the engineers, the nurses, and the librarians?"

"Untrained in the police field, at any rate."

"I'm sorry," Helma said. She wasn't lying. He'd asked her if she remembered what was on the paper, not if she possessed a copy of it. "Now you keep your part of the agreement," she reminded him.

Chief Gallant looked out over the water. "We don't know as much as we'd hoped to by now. We've yet to make a positive identification on the man found in your friend's car. You were right about the rental car. It was parked in a clump of trees just beyond the railroad switching tracks. It appears the latest victim was shot inside it."

"As the driver or a passenger?" Helma asked.

"Most of the blood was on the driver's side. Does that mean anything to you?"

"Just curious."

"You *are* a most curious person, aren't you?" he asked, smiling.

"An inquiring mind is a prerequisite for a good librarian," Helma told him. "Do you suspect there's a connection between this murder and the Ernie Larsen murder?"

Chief Gallant rubbed his chin, smiling at a kayaker,

paddle turning, who followed the rocky shoreline.

"There might be," Chief Gallant said carefully.

"You must admit it's unusual to have two unsolved murders of two strangers within so short a time."

Helma's telephone rang. "Excuse me," she said as she got up. *Saved by the bell*, she thought.

"Helm. It's Ruth. Come over and let's get to the bottom of this thing."

"I'm not sure I know what you're talking about."

"This code. Come on over and let's crack it."

"I asked you to keep it for me."

"I *am* keeping it for you. You didn't say I couldn't look at it."

"That was implied."

"Oh, Helmie. You know I'm oblivious to implications."

"When it's convenient."

"Don't be such a fusser. Come on over. You have to get your car, anyway."

Chief Gallant's legs were stretched across the open door. He'd pulled away from the table and moved his chair closer to the glass door, his back to her.

"That would probably be manageable."

"What do you mean, 'That would probably be manageable'?" Ruth asked. "Oooh," she said. "Do you have company?"

"That's correct."

"Is it you-know-who, the L-A-W?"

"Yes, it is," Helma said matter-of-factly.

"Are you going to tell him about the code?"

"No."

"Well, good. Let's have our own little sleuthing crack at it first. I'll see you when you get here."

Ruth hung up and Helma said into the silent telephone, "Thank you for calling. I'll be glad to volunteer my time. Good-bye." Helma returned to the deck. "Now where were we?" she asked as she sat down.

"You were explaining your inquiring mind," Chief Gallant, said, raising his glass toward her. Helma hadn't noticed before how his hair grew down onto his forehead in an exaggerated widow's peak. No wonder he kept a lock combed down across his forehead; he'd appear quite sinister and un–police chief–ish if he combed his hair back to show that pointed triangle.

"I think not," she said, raising her own iced tea glass. "We were discussing the oddity of two unsolved murders in only three days."

"Here we sit," Chief Gallant said, motioning toward Helma to include her, "drinking iced tea on a deck, sitting on summer furniture, acting like it's a sunny, warm day. If this were California, we'd be inside huddled around a heater."

"Don't you think humans are like most of mammalian life," Helma asked, "adapting to their surroundings as necessary? Are you cold? Would you like to go inside?"

"No. I'm perfectly comfortable. It was just a general observation. I grew up in Indiana. Hot, muggy summers and ice cold winters. When I first moved here I waited two years for summer before I realized that I wasn't experiencing 'off' years; there just isn't much seasonal change."

Helma thought of the way the seasons fell like curtains in Michigan, marking the year's passing, stirring seasonal rhythms with breathtaking clarity.

Once, a few years after she'd moved to Bellehaven, Helma had been intently reading a biography of Thomas Jefferson, deeply caught up and wondering just how much she should believe about Jefferson and this Sally Hemmings, when a noise disturbed her. She'd looked up toward her window, pulling herself away from her book. For the briefest of moments, less than a second, she'd glanced at the gray sky and wondered, *Is this spring or fall?*

Sometimes that instant's confusion came back to her and she found it disturbing. During her first years in Bellehaven, she'd had a vague awareness of living in a state of suspension, as if the natural progression of her life had come to a halt and wouldn't resume until she once again experienced those time-marking seasonal changes of the Midwest.

"Sometimes I like to drive through the farms in the valley; it reminds me of home," he said. "Do you ever get homesick? We could . . ."

"I don't think we're addressing the situation at hand," Helma gently reminded Chief Gallant.

He pulled his chair closer to the table, dragging it behind him from a half-seated position.

"There's no way to actually address the situation, Miss Zukas. You're probably as informed as I am. We have two unsolved murders, as you stated, and unfortunately, you seem to have become involved through accidental association. The more we cooperate, the faster these crimes can be solved."

"Are you implying that I'm not being cooperative?" Helma asked.

"You've been most cooperative. I realize it's very difficult and disturbing to view a corpse laid out in a morgue. All I'm saying is that I hope you'll think about the details surrounding your brief association with these men. What may seem unimportant or trivial or uninteresting to you, might actually be a vital clue."

"I'm sure I've told you everything that could be of any assistance," Helma assured Chief Gallant.

"I appreciate that," Chief Gallant said. He set his empty glass on the table, brushed his hands together, and placed them on his knees, ready to rise.

"You must have checked the agency in Seattle where the deceased rented his car," Helma said. "Did he use an alias?"

Chief Gallant nodded. "From a stolen credit card. You can't write a check without six different kinds of identification, but pull out a piece of plastic and the world parts a path for you."

"Did you have any success with the fingerprints you took from my apartment?" Helma asked.

Chief Gallant shook his head. "The only fingerprints—and there were very few we found—were your own. You keep an impeccably clean home."

"Thank you. And what about the man who was murdered in the library? What did you discover about him?"

Chief Gallant's gaze was too steady on her face. "Not much of importance."

Helma crossed her arms and regarded the chief. "I think you're keeping something from me," she said.

"I could say the same about you, Miss Zukas."

They studied each other, tight-lipped.

Miss Zukas coughed. "Well, I do remember that the deceased man seemed to leave Saul's Deli more because he saw me than because there weren't any tables."

Chief Gallant nodded. "He wanted to avoid you?"

"My feeling was that he didn't want me to see him. I'm sure he heard me call out to him."

Helma nodded toward the chief, raising her eyebrows.

He scratched his chin and said, "We did discover that Ernie Larsen was from Chicago," he said.

"Chicago? As a child or just recently?"

"Recently."

"What else?" Helma asked. She sensed there was more. Chief Gallant's eyes went cool and polite. He was finished sharing any police business with her.

"That's an interesting name: Zukas," he said. "Is it Greek?"

"Lithuanian," Helma told him.

"Lithuanian?"

"Yes. Is that significant?"

"No. It's just not a common nationality."

"Maybe not in this part of the country, but it is where I'm from. From what I understand, in Lithuania the name Zukas is the equivalent of Johnson."

"Were you always last to be called on in school?"

Helma nodded. "My cousin and I, except for part of eighth grade when Roger Zylster moved to town. Being last gave me time to think before it was my turn."

Chief Gallant laughed.

"Do you still have my home phone number?" he asked at Helma's door.

"Yes."

"I'll be ready to hear any facts you recall. Don't hesitate to phone me."

"Certainly."

Helma took a clean white pair of socks from her bureau and sat on the edge of her bed to put them on before she walked to Ruth's.

As soon as she sat down, she felt like Dorothy in the poppy fields outside Oz. A nap. She wanted a nap more than anything in the world. To close her eyes and curl between her flowered sheets. And sleep. It was an unbearable need. Her hand was pulling back the spread before she firmly ordered herself to drop it, to take her socks to the living room and put them on there.

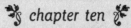

chapter ten

HELMA AND RUTH ASSESS THE SITUATION

"**H**old your horses," came Ruth's muffled shout from inside her house. "I'm on my way!"

She flung open her door, towering, demanding angrily, "How many times do you have to ring that damn thing?"

"What are you talking about?" Helma asked. "I only rang once."

"Once? It was more like ten times. I was changing clothes and couldn't just drop everything, so to speak, to answer the door."

Except for her black turban, which tipped over her right ear, Ruth's black ensemble had been replaced by a pair of faded and paint-splattered jeans and an oversized red T-shirt that read, "SAVE THE WHALES— COLLECT A WHOLE SET," across her chest. The toenails of her bare feet were painted vermilion.

"Only once, Ruth. I rang the doorbell once."

Ruth unpinned her turban and stepped outside, glancing up and down her sidewalk. Then she grabbed Helma by the arm and pulled her inside, slamming the door.

"Somebody rang the doorbell at least ten times," she whispered sotto voce. "Do you think it was THEM?"

"Who is THEM?"

"You know, the killers." Ruth made machine gun motions with her hands, spraying imaginary bullets around her kitchen.

"I find it hard to believe that killers would ring your doorbell and politely wait for an answer."

Ruth finished unwinding her turban. Her dark hair bushed out like an overused toothbrush.

"That's what you think. Real killers are probably forced to do whatever you'd least expect. But *somebody* rang the doorbell a jillion times," she said stubbornly. "You must have scared them off."

"Should we take a look around outside?" Helma asked.

Ruth ran both hands through her hair. It flattened against her head and then sprang out again.

"Oh, forget it. Maybe it was kids or my imagination. Viewing corpses tends to put me on edge." Ruth held up the envelope that Helma had given her for safekeeping. One end was raggedly torn open.

"Do you want to go back to your apartment with the code or should we tackle it here?" she asked.

Ruth's kitchen was in the same disorder as that morning. Her robe hung over the back of the chair where Helma had placed it. The stacks of magazines and letters Helma had arranged sat tidily on Ruth's kitchen table, surrounded by chaos. She grimaced as Ruth's gray cat ran across the room and disappeared into the living room. Cats weren't her favorite animal.

"We still don't know if it's a code," Helma said, "but I'd be happy to give you a ride home if we go to my apartment."

"Oh, Helm," Ruth sighed. "Sometimes you can turn obliqueness into an art form. Let me get my jacket. And I can walk home when we're done."

Helma cautiously checked her Buick before she unlocked the doors: the floors, behind the front seat.

"This car," Ruth said, shaking her head.

"What about it?"

"It's in mint condition."

"Thank you."

"You misunderstand me, Helm. It's un-American. This car should be a junker driven by a seventeen-year-old high school dropout. But there isn't a stain, scratch, or dent on it. The carpeting's not even nappy."

"There's no sense in not taking care of something just because it's old."

Ruth fingered the clear plastic-bubbled seat covers. "How long have you had these on?" she asked.

"Since my parents gave me the car."

"But that was high school graduation. Don't you yearn for a newer car, or even a different one?"

"What for?"

"Oh, Helm."

"Helma," Helma corrected.

As they drove down the winding streets toward the Bayside Arms, Ruth asked, "Did you read Nancy Drew when you were a kid, or Trixie Belden?"

"No, I never did." She braked at a stop sign at Duncan Street, six blocks from Ruth's house. A paper boy with an empty paper bag over his shoulder sat on his bike eating a candy bar. Ruth rolled down her window.

"Hey, kid," she called. "What are you doing down here? Where's my paper?"

The boy grinned, showing silver braces. "Hi, Miss Winthrop. Your paper's probably still in the box. This is Saturday; it's a morning paper. I'm out collecting."

"In that case, skip my house." She laughed out the window and the boy blushed. Helma pulled away from the stop sign with Ruth waggling her fingers good-bye at the paper boy.

"Cute kid," she said, rolling up the window.

"That's exactly what he is," Helma reminded her. "A child who's . . ."

" . . . young enough to be my son," Ruth finished for her. "Don't lecture, Helm dear. Harmless flirting is an age-old rite that defies all bounds of decrepitude. I had a seventy-six-year-old aunt who could blink her eyes at some fresh-faced twenty-three-year-old and have him fall worshipfully at her feet."

Helma didn't doubt it.

"Back to your childhood reading habits, Helmie," Ruth said. "What about the Hardy Boys?"

Helma shook her head.

"Say no more," Ruth said. "I can envision it now. You graduated from Beatrix Potter and 'Mary Had a Little Lamb' directly to Gibbon and Shakespeare."

Helma pulled into the Bayside Arms, aiming precisely for her parking slot.

"That's hardly fair, Ruth. My reading progression was similar to every child's. I even read Sir Arthur Conan Doyle."

"Really!" Ruth arched her eyebrows. "Shall you be Sherlock or Watson?"

"I doubt if we'll progress far enough to consider role-playing. This is a police matter."

"Then why didn't you tell Chief knight-in-shining-armor Gallant that you had a copy of the missing mystery script?"

"I might inform him later. In fact, I fully intend to."

"Are you trying to get a jump on the police with this thing?"

"Certainly not. I don't see what harm there is in waiting a day or two." She hesitated. "Do you ever think the police seem *overly* proud of their training?"

"I detect a little fifth grade rivalry here, Helma."

"That's silly. If we feel we're treading on police-only territory, then of course we'll turn the entire matter back to the police without a second's hesitation."

"Of course," Ruth said.

Helma stepped into her apartment ahead of Ruth, glancing quickly around the kitchen and dining room. Everything was in its proper place.

Ruth removed the folded envelope from her pocket, pushed the organizational behavior book to the edge of the dining room table, and opened the envelope.

Helma tore two sheets of paper from the pad beside her telephone and took two finely sharpened pencils from her ceramic pencil holder.

"Thanks," Ruth said absently, inserting the sharpened end of her pencil between her teeth as she studied the series of letters and numbers.

Helma sat down beside her. Ruth raised her head, blinking. "Write this down," she ordered Helma. "SQ VILKE HCR."

Helma dutifully repeated the letters aloud as she printed them in block letters across the top of her paper.

"Let's work on the letters first and then we'll try the numbers," Ruth said past the pencil in her mouth. It was marked with toothprints, like corn on the cob. "SQ might be an abbreviation for 'square,' or maybe 'squat.' "

"It could mean Southwest Quadrangle," Helma said.

"So what about VILKE?"

"*Vilkas* means wolf in Lithuanian."

Ruth rolled her eyes. "Give me a break."

"It does. I used to know a nursery rhyme about a wolf chasing a squirrel," Helma said. "*Vilkas viel . . . Vilkas bais . . .* I can't remember it." She felt a stab of grief for the lost rhyme.

"Helma, dear. You're blathering again. HCR sounds like some kind of a medical procedure, doesn't it? 'Uncle Pete had an HCR on his liver.' " Ruth shook her head. "No, I think we're on the wrong tack. Think of all your old Girl Scout codes."

"I was never a Girl Scout," Helma said.

"Of course you weren't. Think of all the codes Sherlock Holmes broke."

"I did have to locate a book on cryptography for a patron not too long ago and I recall a few of the more simple ones."

They sat shoulder to shoulder with the paper between them on the table. Helma smelled Ruth's muskiness, a dark expensive perfume mixed with the smell of Ruth's house. Helma slid a little farther away on the seat of her chair. She didn't dislike being close to Ruth; it was just that Ruth seemed to take up so much more room than her body did. She *needed* more room.

"I remember several that used numbers."

"No help here, unless these other numbers are connected in some way," Ruth said.

"There's a transposition code called the rail-fence code that divides the letters into columns so you can easily read the message. Let me show you."

Helma took the paper and wrote:

RTSAHRSED
UHFTEIDAX

"Or," she said, "in its secret form: RTSAHRSEDUH-FTEIDAX."

"I don't get it," Ruth said, frowning at the paper.

"Read the columns from the top down," Helma instructed.

"*Ruth's father is dead*," Ruth read. "Helma Zukas!"

"It's only for illustration," Helma said. "You can make the message into any number of columns. That message is called a 9×2. The multiplication table number used is based on the total number of letters in the message. For this message, you could use whatever results in the number eighteen."

"I can't even balance my checkbook," Ruth said.

"Think about it for a moment. What other multiple results in eighteen?"

Ruth scrunched up her face. "Well, three times six, obviously."

"Correct," said Helma. "That would make six columns of letters, each with three letters. There are others."

"One at a time, puh-lease. My brain isn't used to this sort of orderly thinking." Ruth counted off the letters in front of her. "Ten," she said. "There are ten letters in this gobbledygook, if we ignore the spaces between the letters. Should we?"

"For now," Helma said. "Ten letters leaves us with 5×2 or 2×5."

"I'll do 2×5, and you do 5×2," Ruth said, already mapping out her columns.

Ruth finished first. She crossed her eyes at Helma. "I don't think this is it," she said and passed the paper to Helma. It read, "SKQEVHICLR."

Helma wordlessly passed her sheet to Ruth. Hers read, "SVLECQIKHR."

"There *are* variations," Helma explained. "The letters can be reversed or read diagonally." She tapped the line of letters. "Sometimes a letter stands for another letter, maybe one or two off in the original alphabet, or the actual message can be encoded in the letters by the use of a pattern, such as every other letter followed by every third letter, back to every other letter, et cetera."

"*Et cetera* is right," Ruth said, putting her chin in her hand. "I have a feeling *et cetera* could go on *ad infinitum*."

"You're the one who insisted we try to decipher these letters," Helma reminded her. "We should at least attempt to finish what we began."

Ruth groaned, but bent over her sheet of paper. They worked in silence, occasionally mumbling to themselves.

Finally, Ruth leaned away from the table, stretching her arms above her head. "Why don't we each write down all the words that make some kind of sense, no matter how we came up with them, and see what we have?"

Helma tore off more paper and once again they bent over their lists, each transferring her words to a clean sheet. When they were finished, they set them side by side and silently read the two lists: LIKE, HER, LIVE, VILE, CLIVE, CHIVE, VISE, RICE, CHRIS, RISE, SIRE, EVIL.

"This is pretty pathetic, isn't it?" Ruth asked, crinkling the corner of her paper.

"E, T, A, O, N, R, I, S, and H make up seventy percent of the letters used in the English language, but there's no duplication of letters here so that doesn't help."

"Face it," Ruth said, waving her hand. "We could make these ten letters say anything. They could be the first four words of an e.e. cummings poem." She rubbed her eyes. "My mind won't function on this stuff anymore. These letters look like chicken scratches. What about the dates?"

"March 10 and April 7."

"Where's your calendar?"

"I've already looked. They're both Thursdays and I couldn't discover anything of significance that happened on those dates."

"Both Thursdays. Well, that's significant to *somebody*, I guess. And the numbers?"

"I think they're telephone numbers," Helma said, picking up the paper with the two sets of four numbers: 1649 or 1469.

"How do you know? Did you call them?" Ruth asked.

"Well, actually I did. I made a list of the local exchanges and then phoned each set of numbers with a fabricated story about a letter found in the library."

"My, but you *are* a clever girl."

The telephone rang.

"Miss Zukas?" the voice said after a throat-clearing cough.

Helma recognized Mr. Upman's voice, but she noncommittally said, "This is she."

He cleared his throat again. "This is Albert Upman. I hope I'm not calling at an inopportune time."

"How are you, Mr. Upman?"

Ruth put her hand to her forehead and rolled her eyes at Helma. Helma turned her back to Ruth.

"I'm fine, thank you." He paused. "I want to apologize if I behaved boorishly at lunch today. I didn't mean to offend you. It was just that . . ." he trailed off into silence.

"That's quite all right, Mr. Upman. We all have moments of discomfort during social situations. Please don't concern yourself."

"Thank you."

Helma waited patiently through another long pause.

"I was wondering if you . . . if you might like to hear the Philadelphia String Quartet with me next Wednesday. They're in town for just one performance."

"Mr. Upman . . ." Helma began.

"Just to the performance," Mr. Upman interrupted, rushing his words. "I could pick you up at seven and bring you home immediately after. I would be very honored if you would accompany me."

Helma twisted the phone cord around her finger. What harm could it do?

"I've been wanting to hear the quartet perform for quite some time, Mr. Upman," Helma said. "Thank you for the invitation."

Behind her, Ruth giggled.

"I'm very pleased to hear that, Miss Zukas, Helma. I'll pick you up at seven o'clock on Wednesday, then. And, please, call me Al."

"At seven o'clock. Good-bye," Helma said, still unable to bring herself to say "Al."

Ruth was doubled over in her chair, hugging her stomach and rocking back and forth. Helma pulled her chair a few inches farther from Ruth and watched, waiting for her to stop.

"You're going out with old Uppie!" Ruth burst out.

"I'm merely accompanying him to a performance of the Philadelphia String Quartet," Helma said stiffly. "Perhaps you could share the humor with me."

"Oh, Helm," Ruth said, straightening and wiping the back of her hand across her eyes. "I'm sorry. I don't mean to make fun. You used to be so negative about the man."

"Let's say I've progressed from negative to neutral."

"He's not a bad sort, really. He can come on a little oily at times. I don't think he knows how to meet women. He probably follows a formula he read in a book."

"He told me about his wife," Helma said.

Ruth nodded. "He keeps a picture of her in his wallet. Shows it off like the new baby. She didn't look like the type who'd let a little cancer stop her."

"Ruth," Helma admonished.

Ruth shrugged. "Like I said, he's not a bad sort. I guess he had a heart attack before he moved here and now he's dedicated to exercising and running every day. If you get your body into top shape, cold showers probably aren't sufficient to stifle the primal urges."

Ruth suddenly leaned forward, her eyes bright. "Helm. Just think. If you and Uppie get . . . you know, you and I will be like blood brothers, the seminal sisters, so to speak." She collapsed back in her chair, guffawing and clapping her hands.

"I don't find that humorous."

"I've never been to his house, but he has a boat, you know. The rocking of the waves can . . ."

"I'm really not interested in your personal exploits, Ruth," Helma said coolly.

"I don't know anyone who is," Ruth said sadly and put her hands behind her head, rocking back on the chair legs. "Well, anyway, let's get back to the business at hand. Tell me about the telephone numbers."

Grateful for the change of subject, Helma explained to Ruth how she'd phoned each telephone number and told each person who'd answered the story of the found letter.

"And they believed you?"

"There was no reason not to believe me."

"I suppose not."

Then she told Ruth about the number that was answered by the same voice saying, "yes?" and nothing else, followed by the metallic click in the background.

"But you couldn't tell what made the sound? Not even a guess?"

"Only that it was metallic. There was one other thing. Not long after I called the number, I received a phone call with no one on the other end, but I heard the same metallic click on the line."

"How could anyone have known to phone you? They wouldn't know your number."

"These are modern times," Helma reminded Ruth. "Since the breakup of AT&T, there have been competitive advances in the field of communications. There are telephone systems that trace calls instantly, screen calls from specified phone numbers, and even make automatic calls for you."

"Will wonders never cease?" Ruth said. "Let's call the number." She stood and reached for Helma's phone.

"You go to the phone in my bedroom," Helma said, pulling the phone toward herself, "and I'll dial the number from out here. That way you'll be able to hear it."

Ruth sauntered down the hall to Helma's bedroom. Helma tidied up the table, setting aside their scribbled paper, aligning the pencils.

"Re-uh-dy!" Ruth called. "Dial away!"

Helma dialed the number: 676-1649.

"Yes?" came the soft man's voice. Helma listened intently. She was sure it was a recording; it was identical to the other times she'd dialed the number. She heard breathing but recognized it as Ruth's: too close, too excited.

Click. It came, metallic, clear.

"I heard it!" Ruth shouted into the phone.

Helma dropped the receiver back onto its cradle and ran to her bedroom. Ruth lay on Helma's bed with her feet on the bedspread, smiling at Helma, the phone still to her ear. Helma put her finger to her lips and took the receiver from Ruth's hand, replacing it on its cradle.

"What's wrong?" Ruth asked, sitting up.

"We don't need to announce ourselves to whoever's on the other end," she said. "They could be recording our voices."

"Of course they were recording our voices. Come on, Helm. It's just an answering machine and the click's the signal to start talking."

The phone rang.

"I'll answer it in the kitchen and then you pick it up. But be quiet," Helma warned.

"Hello?" Helma said calmly.

There was silence. Helma held her breath and waited. Finally it came. Click. She carefully replaced the telephone and returned to her bedroom. Ruth was just replacing her phone on the cradle, frowning as if it had betrayed her.

"That's spooky, Helm. I don't think I like it. With all that modern equipment you were telling me about, they may have already dispatched a car to pick us up. Maybe take us for a little ride and dump us into the bay with blocks of concrete tied around our ankles. Let's call Chief Gallant."

"Not yet," Helma said. "Let's wait until . . ."

The phone rang again. Helma and Ruth looked at each other.

"Oh, oh," Ruth said. "I think they're on to us."

"I'll answer it in the kitchen. You listen, but be quiet."

"Hello?" Helma said.

"Oh, Helma dear. I have some news for you. And I wanted to see if you and the dear chief had a nice visit. Did you make any plans for getting together in the future? Don't you agree that he's the sweetest man?"

Ruth's breathing on the other telephone rose in intensity. "Mother," Helma said, cutting in.

"Yes, dear?" Lillian asked. Then she gasped. "Oh, Wilhelmina! Am I being indiscreet? Do you have company? Is he still there?"

"Yes, I have company. May I talk to you later?"

"Of course, darling. You hang up now. What I had to tell you can wait. I'm so sorry. I hope I didn't intrude?" she ended hopefully.

"Not at all, Mother. Good-bye."

After her mother hung up, Ruth's voice exploded into Helma's ear.

"Wilhelmina! Do you and the chief have something going?"

"Don't be overimaginative, Ruth."

"Was he here today?"

"Yes, briefly this afternoon."

"Business or pleasure?"

Helma pulled the phone away from her ear and looked at the receiver. "This is absurd, Ruth," she said. "Hang up the phone and come out here."

"Okay, 'fess up," Ruth said, entering the living room. "What was the chief of the whole goddamn police force doing here in your apartment?"

"He was curious as to how I knew about the rental car, that's all."

"Sweet little Officer Lehman tried to grill me on that very subject when he dropped off my boot. That's one cop who's eager to advance in the world of blue. Now share the facts; what's with you and the chief?"

"Nothing."

"Wilhelmina Zukas! You're blushing!"

"I'm not."

"Are too."

Helma didn't answer.

"Okay. You're not," Ruth said. She opened Helma's refrigerator. "All this intrigue has made me thirsty. Don't you have anything to drink, Helm?"

"Helma. There's iced tea, milk, or diet 7-Up," Helma told her.

"Anything with caffeine or alcohol?"

"Tea contains sixty milligrams of caffeine per five-ounce cup compared to coffee's eighty to one-hundred milligrams."

"It's not the same. Tea is too . . . pale. Why don't we go get a drink? I'll buy."

"No, thank you."

"What's this?" Ruth asked.

"What?"

"This box on the bottom rack. It's got your name and address on it."

"Nothing."

"Hey! It's from your brother Brucie."

"Stay out of it, Ruth."

"I wanta see what's in it."

"Ruth," Helma warned.

Ruth rose from behind the refrigerator door holding the cardboard box. The lid was open and she held it to her nose, inhaling deeply.

"Helma! You sneak. It's a care package from home. Greedy, greedy."

Ruth lifted out a grease-spotted white package. "How often does Bruce do this?"

Helma shrugged. "Every few months. Whenever he gets to Chicago."

"Rye bread, cheese, sausage. It's Lithuania-in-a-box. What's this greasy potato stuff with the globules of fat called?"

"*Kugelis.*"

"That's right: *kugelis.*" She pulled out a shiny brown biscuit. "What's this?"

"A bacon bun."

Ruth took a bite. "Mmm. Potent." She held up a half link of sausage. "Not much left in here, Helmie. If I were you, I'd make an appointment with my cardiologist. The lard in this stuff must be backing up your arteries something awful."

"According to some theories, eating the food of my ancestors can only make me *more* healthy."

Ruth closed the box and put it back in the refrigerator. "Don't count on it," she said. She took another bite of the bacon bun and reached back into Helma's refrigerator for the can of 7-Up.

"You should store that popcorn *in* the refrigerator, not on top of it," she said.

"That's a persistent piece of misinformation," Helma told her. "Popcorn dehydrates in the refrigerator. It's much better to store it at room temperature in a closed container."

"Well, I'll be sure to tuck that little tidbit away for future use." Ruth popped the tab top on her diet 7-Up.

"Don't you want a glass for that?"

"Nah, you'd just have to wash it," Ruth said. With her head back, she took a long open-throated swallow from the can of 7-Up. "What do you think would happen if we made the call to that weird number from another telephone? Like maybe mine?"

"A pay phone might be more prudent," Helma said, thinking that somewhere a computerized machine was doing stealthy calculations and who-knew-what-else with her personal telephone number.

"Great idea, Sherlock," Ruth said. "There's one by the park entrance, isn't there?"

Helma nodded. "We can walk to it."

A warm wind had come up from the south and the early evening air was fragrantly gentle. The phone booth stood at the top of the park, just off the boulevard. The black telephone book holder gaped empty. Helma preferred to use the newer stands without doors or walls. Booths always smelled like they'd been used as bathroom facilities.

"Dial the number, but don't say anything," Ruth said. "Just listen."

"Do you have a tissue?"

Ruth felt in her pockets and pulled out a fuzzed Kleenex. Helma wrapped it around the receiver so she didn't have to touch it. Ruth shook her head at her.

She pushed the buttons: 676-1649, and held the receiver away from her ear so they both could listen.

"We're sorry. You have reached a number that has been disconnected or is no longer in service. If you feel . . ."

"You must have dialed the wrong number," Ruth said.

"It took my quarter, too."

Ruth reached in her pocket and handed Helma two more.

Helma pushed the buttons again, saying each number aloud as Ruth watched.

"We're sorry. You have reached a number that has been . . ."

Helma hung up the phone and stepped outside the booth.

"Let me try it," Ruth said, holding her hand out for the last quarter.

Ruth balanced the receiver on her shoulder and plugged her other ear with a finger. She dialed and listened and frowned and hung up, then hit the coin release button with her thumb and futilely felt in the coin return for their lost quarters.

"They certainly managed that in a hurry. It takes me three weeks to even get an answer from the phone company," she said, leaning her back against the wall of the phone booth.

"Maybe it's not really disconnected at all," Helma said. "Maybe that's why our quarters weren't returned: it's another recording."

"So we'll *think* it's disconnected and stop bothering them?" Ruth asked.

In the park below them a few people strolled or jogged around the paved sidewalk that circled the park. A man leaned over the railing on the boardwalk, staring into the water. Above, a bright green kite hung steadily in the air, its tail made up of multicolored plastic streamers.

"What should we do?" Ruth asked.

Helma pointed down at the park. "Let's walk once around the park. I think more clearly when I'm walking."

Ruth glanced at her watch. "The sun will set pretty soon. I don't want to walk home in the dark."

"I'll give you a ride. It'll only take fifteen minutes to walk around the park and be back at my apartment."

"If I walked as much as you, I could get back into those pants I gave to Good Will last month."

"It would have been more economical," Helma agreed.

The patchy sky portended a colorful sunset. Carloads of sunset viewers were making their way into the park. When Helma had first moved to Bellehaven she'd been amazed at the number of people who "came out" for the sunsets, parking along the high edges of the boulevard, perching on the rocky shore and sitting on the grass to wait for the sun to dip behind the islands. Oohs and Aahs sounded as the pinks and golds rose across the sky, like crowds watching Fourth of July fireworks. The sunsets in Bellehaven were deceptively close, touchable.

"Supposing," Ruth said, waving her arms as she spoke, "supposing this telephone number is a message center of some kind."

"Why go through all the machinations of calling numbers back? Why not just take the message on the answering machine?"

"It could be a double check," Ruth suggested. "Say it's all mechanical, untouched by human hands. We call them, they call us. Our machine responds to the click in some way and completes the circuit." She threw her arms in the air. "Hell, I don't know. It seems like a lot of work to go through just to pick up your messages. We could be in this way over our heads. What with dead bodies and all. Maybe it's time to call in Chief Gallant. What do you think?"

"Not quite yet," Helma told her. "I want to think about it a little more."

"It's not like you to be so uncooperative with authority, Helm," Ruth said.

"It's not like you to be so timid, Ruth," Helma responded.

In silence they continued their walk around the narrow end of the park, past the cedar-sided rest rooms designed like a lighthouse, around the sculpture of three huge pieces of granite that took no shape or form that Helma could discern.

"Look over there," Ruth said, pointing toward three young men playing hacky sack. "You know who the big one looks like?"

Helma looked. The young men stood facing each other near a picnic table, kicking the little ball to one another with the sides of their feet. The "big one" wore cutoffs and a T-shirt. Big-boned, a broad grin on his wide face. Younger, yet he bore an uncanny resemblance to Helma's father.

"Why, like my . . ."

"Right. Like your cousin Ricky from dear old Scoop River."

"Ricky?"

"Yeah, isn't that weird, even the way he walks."

"Ricky?" Helma repeated.

Ruth crossed her fingers like warding off the evil eye. "You remember dear Ricky, don't you, Helm? Cretinous mutant. Always at the back of the class with us: Winthrop, Zukas, Zukas. The tormentor from hell. The guy who made the mess between you and me over Geoff Jamas?"

It wasn't fair—not a bit—that there be any resemblance between someone like cousin Ricky and her father.

"He's getting married," Helma said.

"No! Whoever tricked him into leaving his mother?"

"One of the Cameron girls."

"Well, that'll sure as hell diminish the gene pool."

People said Ricky was "troubled" because of the way his father died. A tractor accident, everyone, including the paper, had called Uncle Mick's death.

On a balmy April morning, Uncle Mick had looped a rope around his neck and over the branch of an oak tree at the edge of his cornfield and then driven the tractor out from underneath himself.

Helma recalled other deaths when she was a child. Murders called hunting accidents. Wife beatings called falls. Children who were unaccountably clumsy. Unmourned miscarriages. Fires blamed on faulty wiring. Things you knew but didn't talk about or understand how you came to know.

"The only dates you'll ever have, cuz," Ricky had taunted her when he heard she intended to be a librarian, "are the ones you stamp in library books." He'd pantomimed stamping books and said in a high, simpering voice, "That'll be two weeks, sir. Come back and see me in two weeks."

A clown horn beep-beeped behind Ruth and Helma and an elderly man in an electric wheelchair whizzed by, a miniature wind sock bobbing from a long pole attached to his chair.

"Ol' Ricky's getting up there," Ruth said. She paused and grinned at Helma. "I guess if he is, then we must be, huh?"

As Helma braked her car in the alley behind Ruth's house, Ruth said, "Listen, Helm. I'm not sure I agree with you about not telling Chief Gallant about the note and the phone calls. Think about it. If you decide to tell him, I'll stand along with you."

"And if I don't tell him for a while?" Helma asked.

"I'll stand along with you in that, too." Ruth giggled. "The sleuthful seminal sisters solve sinister situations."

In the shadows of the car and the glow of the dashboard, Ruth looked fine-boned, almost fragile. She opened her door and the dome light came on, highlighting her bushed hair and haggard eyes. Helma caught a glimpse of herself in the rearview mirror. Ruth was right. They *were* getting up there.

"Good night, Ruth," Helma said.

" 'Night."

Helma relocked the passenger door and sat in her car, watching until Ruth had successfully navigated the raised willow roots and was safely inside her house.

❧ chapter eleven ❧

SUNDAY MORNING

Sometime after midnight Helma was pulled from sleep by the dream image of cousin Ricky.

"That'll be two weeks, sir," he mocked, his mouth twisted in an exaggerated sneer. "Come back and see me in two weeks."

"Two weeks," she mumbled into her pillow, dismissing Ricky but held by his words.

Two weeks. What was it about two weeks? The words circled, echoed, possessed her the way fragments of tunes sometimes did.

She rolled over and put her hands behind her head. Her bedroom was suffused with pinkish light. After dropping off Ruth she'd stopped at the twenty-four-hour grocery store and bought two plug-in night-lights, one for her bedroom and one for her living room. Unfortunately, the only night-lights the grocery store had in stock were intended for nurseries, so one had the leering face of a clown and the other a daisy with a grinning head where the yellow center should be.

Two weeks.

Helma trusted her subconscious. Her slumbering mind often came to her aid. There was the time

163

she'd gone to bed wondering how to squeeze the oversize art books into the already crowded shelves. When she woke up, there was the answer, perfectly sensible: move the record albums to storage, set up a card file for patrons to browse, and shelve the art books on the record shelves.

Don't think about it, she warned herself. *You'll drive it away. It'll come to you on its own.*

Music drifted through Helma's walls for a few moments and was gone. Saturday night traffic.

Helma slid from between her sheets. Barefoot and in her nightgown, she went to her refrigerator and removed the box from Bruce. Only a single piece of *kugelis* remained. She picked it up with her fingers and bit into the mealy, salty concoction. Chewing, she glanced around her quiet apartment, remembering Friday night: the turning doorknob, the intruder, Chief Gallant's fingerprinting her.

Two weeks.

Ruth's chewed pencil and their fruitless attempts at deciphering the note still sat on her table beside the organizational behavior book.

Helma swallowed the last bite of *kugelis*. She licked the grease off her fingers. She knew what two weeks meant.

That was how long books at the Bellehaven Public Library could be checked out.

She flicked on the light over her dining room table and picked up the organizational behavior book. Four date due stamps in the past year and the last two were March 24 and April 21.

Then she picked up the note with the mysterious letters, dates and numbers. Right there in black and white it said: March 10 and April 7. Exactly two weeks before the last two date due stamps. In order to be due on March 24 and April 21, the book had to be checked out on March 10 and April 7, the dates on the note.

Thursdays. All Thursdays. Ernie Larsen's body had been discovered on a Thursday.

Helma's heart pounded. She sat down, gingerly holding the book with the boring title, knowing it was far more than it appeared. But what? She inspected the covers, back and front; nothing was unusual. She held it to the light and squinted down the spine. She checked the endpapers and the title page for penciled notes. Nothing.

She opened the book on the table and began going through it one page at a time, searching for underlining, highlighting. She examined page 49, the library's "secret page," where an ownership mark was always stamped. Nothing.

She didn't know what it was she held, but the book was connected to the note, maybe even the deaths, she was sure of it. She had to hide it.

Helma pulled *A History of Scotland* from the bookshelf in her living room. It was about the same size. She removed the book jacket and placed it on the organizational behavior book. Then she returned the false book to its place next to *The True Story of the Royal Family* and carried the Scottish history to her back bedroom, where she left it on the bedside table with a pencil between the pages that described Falkland Palace, as if a guest were reading it.

Helma slept fitfully until six-thirty, when she finally gave up and lay in bed with her eyes closed, trying at least to relax her muscles. Telephone calls and books and cold corpses kept intruding into the tranquil pool of green water she was imagining.

What had irrevocably awakened Helma was the startling realization that she might actually be in danger. She'd never been in any danger that she was aware of, not *intentional* danger, not in danger that was *aimed* at her. Someone who was still out in the world had killed two men, or at least one. She was convinced the two deaths were connected, and whoever was out there might believe she was connected in some way, too.

She pulled her sheets up to her nose, breathing her bed's sleepy warmth. Didn't everyone believe they were immortal, unharmable, unstoppable? Even Ernie Larsen and Ruth's dead weasel had probably been convinced that they lived charmed, certain lives, that they'd die peacefully in their sleep after a long and satisfying old age.

When Helma's tossing had finally jerked the sheet out from under the end of her mattress, she pulled her nightgown back down around her ankles and sat on the edge of the bed. There was no sense in lying there any longer.

On Sundays, it was Helma's habit to attend ten o'clock Mass at St. Alexander's. If she didn't waste time, she could make it to eight o'clock Mass instead.

In front of her living room mirror, Helma attached a white circle of lace to her hair with a bobby pin. It was no longer a Church rule that women cover their heads during Mass, but it was a remainder from her Sunday catechism days, when the prize for good behavior was the coveted envelope-shaped plastic packet the nuns handed out so sparingly. Cleverly folded inside each clear packet was a modest lace circle. In Helma's stocking drawer, there were three more unopened plastic packets. She didn't know what else to do with them but wear them.

The backs of gray heads greeted Helma when she entered the wooden church, blessing herself at the holy water font and taking a Sunday bulletin. Beyond the waxy smell of burning candles, she sniffed wisps of lilac perfume and Old Spice. She hadn't been to eight o'clock Mass in over a year and was pleasantly surprised by how few children there were.

"Why do you still go?" Ruth had asked Helma once. "Because I've always gone," Helma had told her.

Helma couldn't concentrate; she tried to follow the Mass in her missal, but somehow she kept losing her place. As soon as her thoughts were invaded by murder and mystery, she resolutely turned her eyes toward the votive candles flickering dreamily in the alcove opposite her, the smell of warm wax like all the Masses of her memory.

As she stood for the gospel she thought about cousin Ricky and his father. Uncle Mick had been younger than Helma was now when he died. In fact, all of them except her father had been close to her own age. She shivered.

"Psst," the old woman behind Helma hissed and she was suddenly aware everyone else was sitting and she was the only person in the congregation who remained standing.

She couldn't find the hymn. She forgot the words to the Our Father. Her missal fell to the floor. It was futile. When the front rows began filing forward for communion, Helma slipped out of her pew and left the church.

The morning hung silent and light; moist haze still hid in the shadowed curves of the bay. Behind Helma, the final "Thanks be to God" rose from the church and spilled into the morning. Righteousness hovered over her shoulders as she hurried to her car.

Helma drove six blocks to the Sunlight Bakery and purchased a single croissant. A line eight people deep stood in front of the spitting and sputtering espresso machine, waiting for their frothy drinks.

"I prefer it in a box," she told the clerk, "not a bag."

"Good morning, Miss Zukas."

Helma turned with her boxed croissant and bumped straight into Chief Gallant. The white Styrofoam box slipped from her hand and Chief Gallant caught it with one swift, economical movement.

He reached out with his other hand and took Helma's arm, steadying her, because suddenly, inexplicably, Miss Helma Zukas was unsteady on her feet.

"Are you all right?" he asked, bending toward her, the dimple appearing.

Helma straightened her shoulders and stepped away from the chief. "I'm fine, quite fine. Yes, I'm all right. Thank you."

"Here's your baked good."

"Thank you."

"Care to join me? Have you been thinking about our talk yesterday?"

"I have to return home. I'm sorry."

"Another time," he said.

"Another time," she repeated, hurrying out the door of the Sunshine Bakery.

While her croissant warmed in her toaster oven, Helma retrieved her Sunday paper from her pot of daisies and cut the red rubber band.

"Second Murder Victim Identified," read the headline above a picture of Chief Gallant consulting with two policemen. It was a grim picture of the chief, not at all the way he looked in person.

Helma folded the paper into thirds and set it neatly beside her place setting. She poured her orange juice and arranged the butter dish and a jar of raspberry jam around her plate.

She removed the croissant from her oven, lifted its pointy edge, and placed a pat of butter beneath it to melt. She sipped from her glass of orange juice. Then she took a deep breath, leaned back in her chair, and picked up the newspaper.

"*Bellehaven's second murder victim in three days has been identified as Calvin Whittington, Police Chief Wayne Gallant announced late Saturday night. Whittington, whose address was given as Los Angeles, and whose occupation was listed as 'entrepreneur,' was indicted for embezzlement in New York in 1981. The case was dismissed for lack of evidence. Police Chief Gallant stated that all leads are being followed and there is no evidence that the murder of Whittington is connected with the library murder on Thursday.*"

Helma quickly skimmed the rest of the article, looking for any mention of her or Ruth. Relieved, she went back to the beginning and read the whole report more thoroughly.

Ernie Larsen from Chicago and Calvin Whittington from Los Angeles. Far-flung distances apart. The book and the yellow slip of paper somehow tied it all together. She didn't know how, but the items had import to someone: the men who were dead—and the person who had killed them.

She fingered the papers she and Ruth had worked on. All she and Ruth had done was rearrange the letters to make words, just like the games they'd played as kids: how many words can you make out of the word, "hospital"? This was beyond them. The connection with the book changed things. It was time to give the information to Chief Gallant. Maybe his "trained" policeman's mind *could* figure it out. She glanced at her bookcase. *A History of Scotland* was still there.

Helma slipped her napkin through the napkin ring and called her mother.

"Oh, Helma. How nice of you to call me," she said with such pleasure Helma guiltily realized it really was her mother who usually did the calling.

"You're still coming for dinner, aren't you?"

"Five o'clock. I'll bring some iced tea."

"All right, dear."

"Mother, I was just thinking of cousin Ricky."

"Do you want me to add your name to the congratulations card I'm sending?"

"No thank you. Does Ricky remind you of anyone?"

"Of course." Her mother sighed. "He's like that whole family."

"Not like Daddy?"

"There *are* similarities, Helma."

"Oh."

Lillian's voice softened. "But I think you might call Ricky a condensed version."

Helma laughed and her mother joined in.

"I was just thinking this morning how glad I am that you talked me into moving here, Helma," Lillian said.

"So am I, Mother."

The clouds over the bay were breaking up. A shaft of light spotted the gray water halfway across the bay, turning it opalescent. It would be a warm sunny day, almost like summer. Helma's kitchen clock read just past noon. It was foolish not to take advantage of a beautiful Sunday like this. She dialed Ruth's number.

"What do you want?" Ruth answered before the first ring was complete.

"Isn't this a bit early for you to be so surly?" Helma asked.

"Don't be snide. I have yet to go to my bed. Inspiration attacked in the night and I am now, you'll be proud to know, halfway through a new canvas: a colorful depiction of the events of the past few days. Lots of reds."

"Have you seen the paper?"

"The Daily Insipid? Not hardly. Why?"

"The victim's name was Calvin Whittington." Helma read Ruth the gist of the article. "The paper didn't give much concrete information," Helma told her.

"Perhaps they're missing one vital piece of the puzzle, Helma dear. Why don't you simply hand that little scrap of paper to the police chief of your dreams? He can't very well solve the crime when you're sitting on the evidence."

"What about your professed intent to stand along with me no matter what I decided to do?" Helma asked.

"Did I say that?"

"Yes."

"Had I been drinking?"

"No."

"Well, it stands then."

"Are you taking a break right now?" Helma asked.

"Just waiting for my ocher to dry. Why?"

"Would you like to go for a walk?"

"Is this one of those 'this-kind-of-weather-can't-last' days?"

"I suspect it might be."

Ruth paused.

"I'm going to dinner at my mother's, so it'll be a short walk," Helma assured her.

"All right. I'm game. When and where?"

"Down by the marina would be nice. I can see several sailboats entering the bay. I'll pick you up whenever you're ready."

"Give me twenty minutes to wash the paint out of my hair."

Ruth stood in her alley, wearing bright red pants that ended just below her knees and a yellow sweatshirt. A purple scarf held back her hair.

"Any new clues?" she asked as she slammed the car door.

"Maybe. I've decided to give the evidence, as you call it, to Chief Gallant tomorrow."

"Well, I know you said I said I'd be loyal true-blue to whatever you decided, but I think that's the smartest decision. That code or whatever might make immediate sense to his trained policeman's mind."

There was that term again. "I hope so," she said.

"And, my dear, he'll be *so* grateful to you for cooperating in this messy little business. Who knows how he'll show his appreciation?"

"You sound like my mother."

"Heaven forbid."

The docks of the marina stretched in grids into the harbor, row upon row of expensive sailboats and motorboats and fishing boats. Gleaming in the sunshine, rigging ringing like monks' bells, subdued voices carrying on the breezes, water lapping, punctuated by the shrill cries of sea gulls. To the west the islands, to the east the mountains.

"Let's just walk the docks," Helma suggested.

They strolled from one dock to the next, pausing to watch two young men sanding teak railings, stepping over sails stretched along the dock, stopping beside a toddler playing with a Labrador retriever next to a sailboat.

"This child should be wearing a life preserver," Helma said to the young woman lounging in the stern of the boat with a beer in her hand.

"I've got my eye on him," the woman said, smiling lazily at Helma and Ruth. She waved her beer at the dog. "And so does Jake."

Helma leaned down and picked up the blond boy under his arms, holding him away from her body. The dog growled.

"Sit!" she said to the dog. It sat uncertainly, whining.

"Hey! What are you doing?" the woman asked, standing abruptly, her sailboat rocking.

Helma handed the squirming boy, his face puckering, across the rail to the woman. "Take this child where you can keep a better eye on him," she said. "Accidents happen in a flash."

The toddler broke into a long howl. The dog jumped aboard, whining and turning in circles in the small space around the woman.

"You've got your nerve," the mother said to Helma as she comforted the child against her shoulder.

"Thank you," Helma said.

Ruth leaned toward the woman. "Excuse my friend," she said. "She lost a child this very way."

"Why did you say that?" Helma demanded when they were out of hearing range.

"I was trying to give you credibility, you goose. In this day and age you don't go around picking up other people's children. You're likely to be arrested for any number of crimes against children: kidnapping, molestation, abuse."

"And if the child fell off the dock and drowned, what would the mother be arrested for?" Helma asked.

"She'd probably sue the marina for not having railings."

Helma gave a rueful laugh.

Ruth stretched out her arms. "I could live down here, couldn't you? Spend the rest of my days puttering around on a boat, all cozied up inside on rainy days, drinking coffee with real cream, smelling the salt air."

"Where would you paint?" Helma asked.

Ruth puffed her cheeks at Helma. "Do you have to be so damn pragmatic? Let me dream without bringing up death and taxes, okay?"

"Miss Zukas!" a man's familiar voice called from behind them.

Ruth and Helma turned together. Mr. Upman hurried up the dock toward them. A duffel bag rested on his shoulder and in his other hand he carried a cooler. A baseball cap that said "Seattle Mariners" protected his bald head. He wore shorts and his legs were tan. He had to frequent tanning salons for that, Helma thought; there hadn't been enough sun in Bellehaven to coax out freckles.

"Hello, Mr. Upman," Helma said. Ruth raised her hand to her forehead in a mock salute.

"What are you two ladies doing on this beautiful day?"

"Just taking in a little fresh air," Ruth answered. "How about you?"

"I thought I'd go for a sail. Can't let these sunny days go to waste."

"You sound like Helma."

Mr. Upman touched his cap to Helma. "I'm pleased to hear that you agree with those sentiments, Helma."

"Waste not, want not. That's Helma. She always gets her money's worth."

"Nothing wrong with that. I admire the person who

takes advantage of the moment. You never know what tomorrow might bring."

"Oh, definitely," Ruth said. "One little logging truck in the wrong lane and it could all be over."

"That's right."

Helma nodded stiffly. Why couldn't Ruth just be quiet?

"Can I invite you two for a sail?" He lifted the cooler. "I have liquid refreshment and enough lunch for all three of us—if no one's ravenous."

"Sure!" Ruth answered.

"I'm having dinner with my mother this afternoon," Helma told him.

"What time?"

"Five o'clock."

Mr. Upman looked at his watch. "It's barely one. I promise to have you back by three. You'll still have time to change and arrive at your mother's relaxed and refreshed."

"Come on, Helma," Ruth urged.

"You can go," Helma told her.

Ruth bit her lower lip. "If you won't go, I won't go."

"It's a beautiful day," Mr. Upman coaxed. "May not get another one like it for weeks."

"Can we really be back by three?" Helma asked.

Mr. Upman set down the cooler and made a Boy Scout sign, holding up three fingers. "Scout's honor. I'd really be pleased if you'd join me." He nodded from Helma to Ruth. "Both of you. It's not often I can share my boat with friends. I'd like to very much."

Ruth raised her eyebrows questioningly at Helma.

"All right. But don't forget: three o'clock."

"Great," said Mr. Upman, smiling broadly. "My boat is just up the line here. Dock H."

He led the way along the dock. Ruth nudged Helma and pointed to the thick muscles of Mr. Upman's calves, pursing her lips in a silent whistle.

Mr. Upman stopped beside a sailboat that Helma judged to be thirty feet long. Blue and white with bright teak rails.

"It looks new," Helma said.

"Thank you," Mr. Upman said, standing beside her and admiring his boat with her. "I've had it two years. It's pretty time-consuming, but I try to take care of it. When I moved out here, I decided that if I was going to live near the water, I should take advantage of it. It took me a couple of years to save the money, but I got exactly the boat I wanted."

He stepped lightly into the cockpit and held a hand out to Ruth and Helma. "Welcome aboard."

The boat rocked as they climbed on. Helma immediately sat on the seat by the wheel.

"Can you sleep aboard?" she asked.

"You bet," Ruth answered.

Mr. Upman's face reddened. "Of course," he said. "Cook, too. Let me open the hatch and you can look around."

"Thank you. I think I'll wait until I have my sea legs."

"How about if I pour that refreshment you were talking about?" Ruth asked.

Helma stayed sitting while Ruth climbed down the ladder to the cabin after Mr. Upman. A couple passed and she nodded and smiled to them, trying to look relaxed, like an accomplished sailor. A sea gull landed on the nearest piling, fussing at its feathers. Helma hadn't sailed in years, since she was a teenager in Michigan. Then, there had been Donald, who'd visited from the East Coast one summer and to whom she'd offered her virginity. They'd sailed his sixteen-foot boat every sunny day they were together. It had been the happiest summer of her life.

Ruth and Mr. Upman emerged through the hatch with a bottle of wine and two glasses. Ruth tossed a cushion to Helma. "Here. Sit on this. Save your posterior."

Helma put it beneath her and leaned back.

"This *is* nice," she said.

"We're not even on the open water yet," Ruth said.

"I know what you mean," Mr. Upman said to Helma. "As soon as I come aboard I feel like I've begun my escape. I can forget whatever's irritating back on land."

"And there's been plenty to forget lately," Ruth said.

Mr. Upman nodded gravely. "The last few days have been tragic for our community. The murders . . ."

"Do *you* think the murders are connected?" Helma asked.

"I've wondered that myself. Despite what our local paper says, I'd have to say that yes, I believe there's a connection. It's simply too unusual for there to be two murders of unknown people here."

"But how?" Ruth asked. "The men were from Chicago and Los Angeles. One was a bum and the other at least a suspicious character. I mean, what's being an 'entrepreneur' mean?"

"They could have been involved in any number of unsavory businesses," Mr. Upman said. "When you look at the entire world, not to mention airplane travel, Chicago and Los Angeles aren't that far apart. I just wish they'd chosen somewhere besides Bellehaven and our library to stage their little melodrama."

He poured two glasses of wine and handed one to Ruth and the other to Helma.

"Thank you. What about you?"

"As soon as I get us out into the bay and the mainsail's up, I'll join you."

"Cheers," Ruth said, and she and Helma clinked their glasses together.

❧ chapter twelve ❧

SAILING ON
WASHINGTON BAY

Helma drowsed in the sun, her head resting against the rail and her eyes closed. Mr. Upman's sailboat slipped through the water, whispering to itself, smooth as a rocking horse, a merry-go-round, a cradle. The boat's movement stirred the wind through her hair; she tipped her head back even farther until the sun soothed her throat with little warm strokes. A tune that ran in time with the sea filled her head, but when she tried to hum it her throat felt lazily numb. Helma opened her eyes and saw the straight arrow of the mast touching the blue sky. It spun dizzily off center. She closed her eyes again.

"Psst, Helma."

"Mmm."

"D'ja feel funny?" Ruth asked, her voice slurring.

Ruth had drunk too much again. Helma sat up to tell her so.

"Ruth . . ." she began. Ruth's face expanded, then contracted, her chin distorting.

Maybe Ruth had drunk too much but Helma knew that she'd only taken a few sips before she discreetly poured the remainder into the bay. Alcohol at midday threw the rest of her day off too much. She squeezed her eyes shut and opened them again.

The entire sailboat, the shimmering water, the trees and hills on the opposite side of the bay contorted as if she were looking into the bowl of a silver spoon. Her head felt too heavy for her neck.

"Oh oh, Ruth," Helma said, trying to hold her head steady.

"What a day," Mr. Upman said from somewhere above her. "This is the first good sail I've had this year."

Helma opened her eyes to his thick muscled thighs.

"You . . ." she said, and could go no farther.

"Is something wrong?" he asked. "Ruth? Helma? What's wrong?"

He knelt on one knee in front of Helma. She felt his cool hand against her forehead. His eyes behind the thick lenses were gigantic.

"Shick," Ruth said and lurched to the back of the sailboat. She leaned her head and shoulders over the railing and heartily vomited.

Helma tried to reach for the bright red pants. Ruth went limp, pitching dangerously across the railing. Helma's hand gripped only air.

"My God!" Mr. Upman cried. Helma dizzily saw him leap forward and grab Ruth by the shoulders. He steadied her, patting her back as she retched.

"Anything wrong?" a woman's voice called. Helma was vaguely aware of a black powerboat alongside. It bobbed, up when Mr. Upman's boat was down, down when his was up. Other boats dotted the bay in wavering confusion: white and brightly colored sails, darting speedboats that duplicated themselves and became singular again, stately cruisers suddenly growing as big as state ferries.

Helma tried to raise her hand, as in school. *Excuse me. Take me off this boat, please. At once.*

"We're fine, thanks," Mr. Upman called back. "She just got a little seasick."

"A landlubber, eh?" a male voice asked, laughing.

"Seems so."

Her hand was too heavy. It fell back into Helma's lap.

The black boat moved out of Helma's vision. It was leaving her. It was gone. Ruth still hung over the stern with Mr. Upman steadying her.

"Are you all right now?" he asked Ruth. "Can I pull you back on board?"

"Reading."

"What?"

"I am reading," came the carefully enunciated words.

Mr. Upman chuckled. "Time to come up for air, I think," he said and hoisted Ruth back into the cockpit.

Ruth rubbed her mouth. "Dishgushting."

Helma felt in her pants pocket for her cotton handkerchief and held it out. "Give her this," she said, averting her eyes from the off-kilter approach of Mr. Upman.

"Thish ish the she wolf," Ruth said as she wiped her mouth. "That'sh itsh name: the *She Wolf*."

"Oh, the name of my boat," Mr. Upman said, sitting down beside Ruth, one hand on the wheel.

"Sea Wolf," Helma corrected, bringing up the words from some dim store, seeing each one in reverse white-against-black as she spoke it. "*The Sea Wolf*—Jack London."

"Are you ill, too?" Mr. Upman asked Helma.

"Dizzy," Helma said. "T's all foggy."

"I'd better take you two back to the harbor."

Ruth slid down on the seat, her head on her seat cushion. The last thing Helma heard was Ruth's gentle snoring mixed with the soothing "swishhh" of water along the sides of Mr. Upman's boat.

* * *

Helma was on her way to visit her dentist on the fourth floor of the Walker Building. Helma didn't ride elevators but she had no choice. An official-looking sign blocked the stairs: Closed. Wet Paint.

Reluctantly she stood in the foyer and pushed the UP button on the elevator.

"Ding!" went the metallic bell, announcing the elevator's arrival.

The black doors smoothly separated and there they all stood, side by side. Jocular, lips parted as if they'd just finished chuckling over a good joke, shoulder to shoulder, filling the elevator, warm and colorful under the overhead lights.

Her own dead father stood in the middle, his face tanned and his hair still too short. Next to him her grandfather and behind him Uncle Mick and Aunt Aldona. In the corner, mischievous Aunt Pansy nudged Uncle Tony in the ribs.

Her father's eyes widened in surprise at the sight of Helma, then crinkled into a moist welcoming smile. He clapped his hands together once, hard, joyously, then raised his hand and beckoned to her.

"Daddy!" she cried out, dropping her purse.

The elevator doors held open. Their similar eyes twinkled. Their cheeks stretched and dimpled. They shifted and grinned and moved closer together, hunching their shoulders and pressing against the walls, making a space at the front center of the elevator between Helma's father and grandfather, just room enough for Helma to press into.

Her father reached out the hand with the deformed pinky, moving to the open door of the elevator, not crossing the space into the foyer. Helma extended her own hand, eagerly at first, then tentatively, stopping just at the lobby side of the line made by the elevator doors, almost touching his fingers.

Her hand faltered. "Daddy," she said again. Helplessly, this time, as the elevator bell dinged.

The doors slid silently toward one another. They all smiled, but sadly now, their beckoning turning to farewell waves. As the doors whispered together her father's brilliant eyes held her own, hungrily looking at her as if he might never see her again.

Helma woke to dreamlike rocking and a low undercurrent of mechanical humming. She grimaced at the pounding tenderness in her head. Where was she? She lay very still, breathing from her diaphragm with her eyes closed: in for the count of four, hold for four, release for the count of eight. Concentrating only on her breath. Five times, ten times. Ten breaths usually did it: this time she did twenty. That couldn't fail.

She opened her eyes on the eighth count of her twentieth exhalation. Tweed fabric and gleaming wood, a round window. A scratchy wool blanket covered her from the neck down. She swallowed and checked to be sure she was fully dressed; she was, down to her shoes and socks. Her mouth was dry and foul, tasting like cheese she'd once eaten that had gone off. She experimentally shook her head and raised herself onto her elbows. She was in the cabin of Mr. Upman's boat.

In the shadowy light, she made out the perfectly spotless galley, the neat charts in their labeled slots, the clean table. Helma held her wrist to the light from the porthole. It was almost eight-thirty.

Eight-thirty! She'd been asleep for seven hours! Her mother was probably frantic. How could she have slept so long? She remembered the dizziness and her wildly distorted vision. She couldn't have drunk that much. And Ruth. Where was Ruth?

Helma balanced herself with both hands and slid off the gently pitching bunk. Black-and-gold streaks of light shot across her vision. She braced herself against the galley counter and her eyes slowly cleared. Her head throbbed, but at least the cabin and the hatch were all in their proper proportions.

The steps were agonizingly steep. Helma crawled up them on her hands and knees and pulled herself through the hatch into the evening light.

Ruth still lay on the molded seat where Helma had last seen her, her head on the cushion and her mouth open. A blanket identical to the one that had covered Helma was draped over Ruth. Helma watched Ruth until she saw her nose twitch.

The sails were down and the boat vibrated with the steady pulsing of its inboard engine. Mr. Upman stood at the wheel, a cigarette in his mouth, facing the lights of the marina. He didn't notice Helma; he stood with one hand on the ship's wheel, relaxed.

The air carried the odor of diesel fuel. Around them, Helma saw other boats, their engines throbbing and chugging. Muted voices carried across the water. They were in a long line of boats, all making their way back to the marina for the night, one after the other. Helma remembered her grandfather's cows swaying one after the other as they plodded along the deep path they'd worn next to the fence line. Returning to the barn at milking time.

She slipped a little on the deck, catching herself on the hatch. Mr. Upman flicked his cigarette into the water and reached out an arm to steady her.

"Helma! Are you feeling better? I'm so sorry. I don't know what happened. All I can figure is that something was wrong with the wine."

"I have a terrific headache," she said, sitting down and rubbing a palm across her forehead. "Why were you spared?"

Mr. Upman grinned sheepishly. "I didn't drink anything. I planned to but when I saw the effect on you two I decided I'd better not."

"Where did you purchase that wine?"

"I don't remember. It's from my own stores. I think I've had it for a while."

Helma tapped her watch. "My mother's probably

beside herself. I was supposed to have dinner with her. Why did you keep us out so long? I distinctly—well, not too distinctly—recall hearing you say you were taking us back to the harbor."

Mr. Upman sat down beside her. "Believe me, that was my intention and I know I should have. But when you both fell asleep, I decided to stay out until you were yourselves again. It seemed the kindest thing to do."

"So we wouldn't be seen, you mean?"

He shrugged.

"And so we wouldn't embarrass the library," Helma said with certainty.

Mr. Upman shook his head. "So none of us would be embarrassed, that's all. I stayed near the channel and I assure you, if I'd had the slightest concern about your state of health, I would have immediately taken you in."

"I appreciate your tactful actions," Helma told him. "I'd better wake up Ruth now."

"She drank more than you did."

"I'm still going to wake her up," Helma said, feeling her way across the cockpit to sit at Ruth's head.

"Ruth," she said, prodding Ruth's shoulder.

Ruth stopped in midsnore and grunted.

"Wake up, Ruth. It's late."

"Oh, God," Ruth moaned and put her hand over her eyes. "What evil have I done?"

"None. But it's late and we're almost to shore."

Helma pulled on Ruth's arm and she sat up, weaving with the boat's gentle forward chugging, letting the blanket drop from her shoulders. She hunched over, her hands covering her face. "I just want to die."

"Not today," Helma assured her.

Ruth lifted her head and in a thick voice, asked Mr. Upman, "Have you done something funny again, like that time we went to your friend's beach house and you asked me to . . ."

"No, I swear it," Mr. Upman said. "You both drank the wine; I didn't. You both, as they say, 'passed out.' I don't know what caused it."

"Killer wine," Ruth mumbled. "That's a new one on me."

Mr. Upman motored the sailboat into its proper aisle and skillfully steered it toward its slip. Around them, evening-softened voices called like retiring birds:

"Catch that line."

"Take the cooler."

"Did you get the keys?"

"Don't forget the life preservers."

Helma and Ruth numbly watched Mr. Upman moor the boat against the orange dock fenders. Helma thought briefly about helping him, then dismissed the idea.

Lights reflected from the oily water of the marina, shimmering to rainbow colors. Through the myriad masts the last of the sunset arced the sky with purple and pink. It had been a beautiful day. Helma was sorry she'd missed it.

Mr. Upman jumped lightly to the dock and lifted his cooler down beside him. He held out his hand toward Helma and Ruth.

"I'll take you home," he said.

Ruth took his hand and wobbled to standing. The boat rocked and Ruth gasped, windmilling her free hand, fighting to catch her balance. Helma reached for her arm and steadied her.

"It's the leasht you can do," Ruth admonished Mr. Upman, slurring a little. "You can also write a tardy excuse for Helma to give to her mother."

On the dock, Ruth dropped down to sit on top of the cooler, elbows to knees.

"I apologize for your missing your mother's dinner, Helma," Mr. Upman said, holding out his hand to Helma. "If you'd like me to explain the situation to her, I'd be happy to."

"No, thank you," Helma told him, balancing herself on the boat railing and ignoring his hand. "I'm quite capable of explaining myself to my mother."

"She's probably already called Chief Gallant, hoping he's got you snuggled somewhere in the back of a police cruiser," Ruth said.

"Oh. I didn't know . . ." Mr. Upman said, one hand raised in anticipation as Helma climbed from the boat to the dock. "Are you and the chief . . . ?"

"Please don't pay any attention. Ruth is being silly."

"Not me. Your mother."

"Ruth!"

"Sorry."

"Shall we go?" Mr. Upman asked.

"Betcha. Lead on," Ruth said, standing shakily and leaning against Helma.

"Let me take your arm," Mr. Upman said, picking up the cooler and reaching for Ruth's elbow.

"No thanks," Ruth told him, jerking her arm close to her body. "You've helped me enough, I think."

"Can you walk?" Helma asked her.

"As well as you."

Mr. Upman led the way. Ruth looked over her shoulder at Mr. Upman's boat and nudged Helma.

"See?" she said. "I wasn't as drunk as you thought."

"What are you talking about?"

Ruth pointed to the stern of the boat. "Old Uppie's boat. Its name *is* *She Wolf*, not *Sea Wolf*. You always have to find some libraryish connection, don't you?"

Helma stared at the dark swirly script across the stern: *She Wolf*.

"Congratulations," she said to Ruth. "You can read."

"Tch, tch," Ruth clucked, leaning more heavily on Helma. "Sarcasm doesn't become you."

Mr. Upman waited for them to catch up. The dock was barely wide enough for two to walk side by side. Whenever they met anyone, Ruth and Helma turned sideways, holding on to each other like dance partners.

The *She Wolf*. Not the *Sea Wolf*, the *She Wolf*. It tickled at her memory.

"I hope you'll come sailing with me again on another occasion," Mr. Upman said. He coughed. "Today didn't work out very well. Next time you can bring the refreshments."

"I'd like to have a talk with you about those refreshments," Ruth said, raising her voice.

Mr. Upman stopped.

"Excuse me," a man behind them said and they squeezed to the side of the dock so he could carry a canvas bag past.

Mr. Upman patted the top of the cooler. "I want you to know that I have the bottle of wine right here and tomorrow I'll take it to the police station to have it analyzed. I'll let you know as soon as I receive the results."

"Fat lot of good it'll do us then," Ruth grumbled.

"Ruth, he can't change what happened. At least we'll know what it was," Helma said.

"Lock the barn door . . ."

"Would you like me to take you to the hospital?" Mr. Upman asked. "It might be a good idea, in case there are more symptoms."

"Forget it," Ruth said. "I'm familiar enough with the symptoms I'm having to know I'm on the road to recovery."

"What about you, Helma?" he asked.

"I'm feeling much better," she assured him.

As they passed the Yacht Club, a woman in a knee-length fur coat stepped through the front door. A young man in suit and bow tie held the door for her. A doorman in Bellehaven.

"Al!" the woman called, raising one hand as if hailing a taxi and tapped toward them on high heels.

"Brenda," Mr. Upman acknowledged. "How are you?"

"Fine, but we'd all be better if you'd stop by more often. Where have you been lately?"

"It's a busy time at the library," Mr. Upman said, passing the cooler from one hand to the other.

Brenda rolled her eyes. Gardenia perfume hovered around her. "Heavens, yes. With murders taking place right under your nose."

In a sweeping glance, the woman appraised Helma and Ruth and dismissed them. They stood in the circle of a mercury light which buzzed and cast a greenish pallor of unnatural brightness.

"The moon is made of green cheese," Ruth unaccountably said.

"Brenda," Mr. Upman said, waving his hand toward Helma and Ruth. "May I introduce you to . . ."

Brenda held up a red-nailed hand. "Not tonight, Al. I have to rush off. You stop by and see me soon, won't you?"

"Of course," Mr. Upman replied, switching the cooler back and forth, back and forth.

Brenda lightly brushed his cheek with the tip of her fingers and kissed the air in his direction. Ruth winked at Helma and said softly to Mr. Upman as they watched Brenda's departure, "That one would eat you up and boil your bones for consommé, Uppie."

Mr. Upman didn't answer. He adjusted his glasses and led them through the parking lot to his compact station wagon. Ruth and Helma got in while Mr. Upman stored his cooler in the back. The car's interior smelled of cigarettes. A spiced air freshener in the shape of a pine tree hung from the radio dial.

"I just want to sleep for two weeks," Ruth said, stretching her legs across the backseat. "Then I'll be willing to live again."

The hatchback of the station wagon slammed, followed by the cool sound of breaking glass.

"Damn," said Mr. Upman.

"What happened?" Helma asked. She opened her

door to get out. Too fast. Blue points of light flashed, turned black, and receded. She squared herself on the car seat again.

Mr. Upman came around to her side of the car, holding his glasses. The left lens was shattered. He squinted at her.

"They fell off when I slammed the back. I stepped on them."

"Do you have another pair?"

"At home."

"I'll drive us," Ruth said from the back.

Mr. Upman shook his head, one corner of his mouth turned up. "If you don't mind, we're only a few blocks from my house. I'll stop by and pick up my other pair. It'll only take a minute."

"Can you see to drive?" Helma asked. "I feel much better now. I could drive you home in my car and then drive Ruth and myself home. I'm much better, really."

"I wouldn't feel right. No matter how you look at it, what happened is my fault. I'll get my other glasses, then take you ladies home. Tomorrow I can drive you down here to get your car."

"But . . ." Helma began.

"Let him do it, Helm," Ruth said. "I think I trust his one-eyed driving more than your inebriated driving."

"I assure you I'm not inebriated," Helma told her. "But Ruth may be right, Mr. Upman; it's probably safer if you drive."

"Thank you." Mr. Upman got in behind the wheel and gingerly placed his broken glasses on his nose, closing the eye behind the shattered lens.

As he backed his car out of the parking place, twisting his neck to see behind them, Helma remembered.

"*Vilkė*," she said aloud, suddenly seeing the word with a dot over the e.

"*Vilkė*?" Ruth asked. "Isn't that one of the words . . ."

"Ruth," Helma firmly interrupted. "Look what you're doing to Mr. Upman's car seat!"

"What?" Ruth squawked, jerking her feet off the seat.

"What did you say, Miss Zukas?" Mr. Upman asked.

"I . . . well, I've forgotten already. I'm sorry."

Vilkė. Vilkas. Wolf. *Vilkas* was a wolf. Wasn't *katė* a female cat? Was *vilkė* the feminine of *vilkas*? Diacritic, an e with a dot over it? A she wolf? She couldn't remember. Her Lithuanian was murky, all so distant.

A pale line of light showed behind the San Juan Islands. Mr. Upman slowly drove along the opposite side of the bay from Helma's apartment building, driving deliberately into the darkening evening, away from the harbor, farther from town and the people in it. She looked longingly across the bay, picking out the banks of twinkling lights that outlined her building.

Helma pulled her hand away from her mouth and held it tightly in her lap. She hadn't chewed her fingernails since she was in ninth grade.

Mr. Upman's boat, the *She Wolf*. *Vilkė*, the word in the middle of the code, meant she wolf in Lithuanian. How could that be? She glanced at Mr. Upman. His head was thrust forward over the steering wheel, one eye closed, his attention on the road. In the backseat, Ruth hummed a two-note tune.

Mr. Upman pulled off Seaview Drive onto a narrower paved road that ended in a cul-de-sac. He pressed a black button on the dashboard and the garage door of a brick and cedar-sided house automatically rose. Lights went on inside a two-car garage.

Mr. Upman pulled his station wagon into the right side. A dark shadow of oil stained the concrete floor. On the left side of his garage stood a small but obviously expensive gym. A chrome-and-black Nautilus machine, a rowing machine, a stationary bicycle. Even a large mirror. Ruth nudged Helma's shoulder and pointed to the photos of muscular men lining the mirror's frame.

"So this is how you do it," Ruth said. "Beats waiting your turn at the health club."

SQ VILKE HRC. Did SQ stand for Squabbly Harbor?

Helma's stomach lurched. Her vision wavered and she had the trapped, out-of-control elevator feeling as Mr. Upman's garage door mechanically lowered behind them, shutting her in.

Mr. Upman turned off the engine and sat staring through the windshield for a few seconds. The garage was silent except for the pinging of the cooling engine. The fluorescent lights on the ceiling buzzed.

"I'd like you to come inside," Mr. Upman said coolly, opening his car door.

Ruth leaned over the back of Helma's seat. She looked at the closed garage door behind them, then at Helma.

"Something about this doesn't feel right, Helm," she whispered.

Mr. Upman opened Helma's door and stood behind it, holding it for her, waiting.

She didn't move. Mr. Upman impatiently tapped his fingers on the car door and leaned back inside the car.

"Miss Zukas?" he politely questioned. The shattered eyeglass obscured his left eye. "Miss Winthrop?"

Ruth sighed and clucked her tongue against her teeth. "Oh, Uppie. What naughty business have you gone and got yourself into?"

❧ chapter thirteen ❧

HELMA AND RUTH AT MR. UPMAN'S HOUSE

"**P**lease leave the car and come into the house," Mr. Upman said in a new, flat voice.

Helma and Ruth climbed out of the car and stood in front of a wooden door. Helma's dizziness vanished. She felt coldly awake. Mr. Upman moved around behind them.

"It's unlocked," he said. "Please go inside."

She hadn't seen a weapon, but it was there, its presence registered in his voice: the confidence that he wouldn't be disobeyed, that note of complete control.

Ice settled inside her, threatening to paralyze her. *Don't think*, she told herself. *Breathe. Look around. Calm water, blank paper.*

Ruth opened the door and they followed one after the other into a narrow hallway. An avocado washer and dryer stood in a laundry room off the hall; an ironing board was set up in front of the dryer. They proceeded through the kitchen, first Ruth, then Helma, followed by Mr. Upman. The kitchen was as spotless as Mr. Upman's library office and the galley of his sailboat. Pans with glowing copper bottoms hung artfully above the stove. The stainless steel sink sparkled.

"Straight ahead," Mr. Upman ordered, close behind Helma.

Along one wall of the living room, floor-to-ceiling windows looked out across the bay. Points of light outlined the shore and the water curved black between them. Restful grays, blues, and mauves blended and complemented each other throughout the room. The walls were hung with paintings and a Coast Salish Indian mask.

"If you ladies will please make yourselves comfortable on the floral love seat," Mr. Upman suggested politely. But Helma knew politeness was not a consideration; it was an order.

A cut glass vase on the rosewood coffee table in front of the love seat held deep purple—almost black—glass tulips, as fragile and lifelike as the real flowers at their peak.

Ruth stumbled nervously, then dropped close beside Helma. "Oh, mercy, mercy," she said in an outrush of breath.

Mr. Upman stood above them, holding a small black revolver.

"What's this all about, Helma?" Ruth asked. "Why does he have a gun?"

"I think he believes we're the women who know too much."

Ruth looked at Helma, her eyebrows arched over her wide eyes. "What is it we know?"

"That's exactly the subject I'd like to discuss with you," Mr. Upman said.

"Cut this out, Uppie. We don't know anything," Ruth said. "I mean, whatever you think it is we know, we don't. Right, Helma?"

"Actually, I think we might," Helma said. "Umph," she grunted as Ruth elbowed her in the side.

"It's too late to pretend ignorance," Mr. Upman said. "I suspected but I wasn't sure until I heard you say 'vilkė' in the car."

"*Vilkė: She wolf*," Helma said.

"How else would you have known unless you had a copy of our dead friend's note."

"How did *you* know?" Helma asked. "Are you Lithuanian?"

"Definitely not. There are dictionaries in the library, Miss Zukas, did you forget? Even dictionaries for peasant languages like Lithuanian."

"But how did he know the word was Lithuanian?" Ruth asked. "It might have been Dutch or Swahili."

"I'd guess the e on the original note was diacritic," Helma told her, "*vilkė* with a dot over the e. And besides, Ernie Larsen was from Chicago."

Ruth snapped her fingers. "Chicago!" she repeated.

Helma nodded. "The home of more Lithuanians than anywhere else outside Lithuania."

"Bingo! So old Ernie wasn't a bum, was he?"

"I'd bet his name wasn't Larsen either," Helma said.

"Excuse me," Mr. Upman said. "Would you mind if I interrupted to ask a question?"

"Be our guest," Ruth invited.

Mr. Upman pointed his gun at her forehead and Ruth sat back, her hands raised.

"Ask your question and then I expect you to turn us loose," Helma said in her best silver-dime voice.

Mr. Upman didn't even blink. "Don't push your luck. If there hadn't been so many witnesses out on the bay today, you two would already be fish food."

"Fish food?" Ruth asked. "That's trite, Uppie. At least say it with a Jimmy Cagney accent."

"So you did put something in the wine?" Helma said.

"Not enough, obviously."

"And you were actually going to *kill* us?" Ruth asked.

He swung the gun toward Helma. "Where's the book?" he asked.

"What book?" Helma asked.

"What book?" Ruth echoed, genuinely puzzled.

Mr. Upman very deliberately moved the gun closer to Helma. He held it there, steadily trained between her eyes. The inside of the barrel was blackest black, a black hole to eternity.

"It's in my apartment," she said.

"Would you mind explaining exactly where."

"Why?"

"It's overdue. I'm sending someone to retrieve it so you won't have to pay a fine, do you understand? If it's not exactly where you say, all kinds of unpleasant things are going to happen."

"It was you in my apartment, wasn't it? You were looking for the book."

"What book?" Ruth asked again. "What's this all about?"

"None of your business," he said. "Continue," he told Helma.

"It's in my bookcase, inside a book jacket from *A History of Scotland*. How did you know I'd even left the library with it?"

"You thoughtfully checked it out to yourself. Now, I find it necessary to make a few phone calls, ladies," he said, waving his free hand toward the archway at the other end of the living room. "Please bear in mind that I can see your every move; it would behoove you to stay exactly as you are."

"Why . . ." Ruth began.

Mr. Upman smiled only with his mouth and pointed the gun at Ruth again.

"I'll be back directly," he said.

Ruth slumped into the cushions. "Our dear old Uppie is no longer our beloved, harmless, people-serving librarian, is he?" She studied the living room. "This is the most anal retentive case of interior decorating I've ever seen. The paintings are the only things that are any good."

Ruth squinted at the walls, then turned to the painting that hung over the love seat behind them.

"God, Helma. I think this is a *real* Chagall."

From farther down the living room wall, a metallic click sounded. A very familiar click. Metal against metal, followed by a swishing noise. Helma leaned forward. On a table ten feet away, between a Greek vase and a large crystal figure of a stag, stood an apparatus of descending chutes which held silver balls the size of marbles. The silver balls descended from one chute to the next, marking the passage of time. Helma had seen similar metallic clocks displayed in gift shops. The balls hitting together made the same click they'd heard on the phone. The recording or whatever it was on the telephone had been made in this house.

"I think we should leave as soon as possible," Helma told Ruth. "The phone calls he's making are probably not to our benefit."

"Good idea, Helma Zukas. We'll just get up and walk out the front door. He's bound to miss one of us with his first shot."

"Getting cozy in here, are we?" Mr. Upman asked, reentering the living room.

"Couldn't find your glasses?" Ruth asked.

Mr. Upman's light eyes regarded Ruth and Helma coolly. Without the glasses and with his normal slightly out-of-focus stare replaced by an icy gaze, Mr. Upman lost his last vestige of harmlessness. He eyed them steadily, no trace of the mild foolishness that Helma frequently associated with Albert Upman. She didn't think he'd be so clumsy with a gun as he sometimes was handling card catalog drawers.

"How'd you do that?" Ruth demanded. "Contact lenses?"

"Be quiet."

"A disguise wasn't necessary to become a credible librarian," Helma said.

Mr. Upman waved the little black gun, motioning to Helma. "I think you'll be more comfortable in the bedroom," he said.

Ruth bounded off the love seat, rising to her full height, her hair wild, her bloodshot eyes wide. "Don't you dare touch her, you two-faced cretin."

Mr. Upman turned the gun toward Ruth, grinning. "Sit down. Don't be a fool. I just think you two ladies might be more comfortable in separate rooms."

"You intend to divide and conquer, is that it?" Helma asked. She tried the silver-dime voice again, disdainful, confident.

"That's dumb," Ruth interjected. "Wouldn't it be easier to keep an eye on us if we were together? That's what I'd do, anyway."

"Down, down," Mr. Upman said, jabbing the gun toward Ruth. "I suggest you seat yourself."

"Ruth is correct, Mr. Upman," Helma said, remaining seated on the love seat. "If we're separated, one of us is likely to attempt an escape."

"I'll be the judge of that. You," he pointed the gun at Helma, "stand up, and you," he pointed at Ruth, "sit down."

Helma and Ruth exchanged places. From his shorts pocket, Mr. Upman removed a strip of plastic with serrated ends like a garbage bag tie. He gave Helma a warning look and set his pistol on the floor beside his knee while he threaded one end of the tie around Ruth's left wrist. With a knife from his other pocket, he slashed a hole in the upholstered arm of the love seat and threaded the plastic strip through it, pulling it tightly around Ruth's right wrist until Ruth was leaning across the arm of the love seat, hugging it. He smiled at Ruth and patted her wrist.

"Comfortable?"

Ruth glared at him and turned her head.

"This way," he said to Helma, walking close beside her, holding the gun at her back.

Off a hallway behind the living room they entered a bedroom decorated in cool lime green and white. Heavy white furniture: a bureau, dresser, and nightstand flanked the king-size bed with its white headboard. Watercolors and drawings hung on the walls. Helma wasn't as familiar with art as Ruth but she guessed that these too were "real."

Mr. Upman pushed her toward a white brocade chair facing the bed. "I'll leave you here to your own entertainment."

"Why are you doing this?" Helma asked.

"I don't believe it's necessary to answer any of your questions."

"676-1649 is your telephone number, isn't it? Not your personal number, but the other number, the recording with the automatic dial-back."

"My, my, but you're a regular Sherlock Holmes, aren't you?"

"There are numerous female sleuths you could compare me to. It's not necessary always to refer to men."

Helma kept her hands to her sides, out of sight, hoping he wouldn't tie her to the chair as he had Ruth.

"You killed Ernie Larsen, didn't you? What were you doing when he surprised you? And then you wore his shoes to make the tracks by the library door so it would appear he knew his murderer, that's why his shoes were untied, isn't it? Exactly who are you, and what's in that book? Were you working with Calvin Whittington? Do you even have a professional library degree?"

"That's enough."

Mr. Upman went to the telephone on the nightstand and disconnected the cord from the wall. He wound it around his hand and carried the phone to the door.

"Just for your own information, there are no hidden weapons in this room. The window doesn't open, and the door will be locked from the outside."

"Bedroom doors usually lock from the inside," Helma pointed out.

Mr. Upman laughed. "You have a compulsion to correct everyone, no matter the circumstances, don't you? I can assure you that because of the oddities of inferior construction, this particular bedroom door locks from the outside."

"Wait. Why did you bother with the disguise? The phone calls?"

"Even crime can be embellished to make it more interesting."

"What are you going to do with us? At least tell me that."

Mr. Upman stood in the open door. "That will be decided shortly. Be patient, please." And he closed the door.

Helma rose from the brocade chair and tried the doorknob. It wouldn't turn. She searched the room, beginning with the bureau and dresser. The drawers were empty except for white tissue paper linings, not even a pair of socks. The dresser was the same. Only a lamp with a padded fabric base and the polished white shell of a sand dollar stood on the nightstand. If this wasn't the guest bedroom, Mr. Upman had very recently made a decision to move.

He was right. There was nothing she could use as a weapon. The window had either been painted shut or the construction had been off-center and the sash was out of alignment. Maybe it, too, was locked from the outside. She pushed upward, straining, but it didn't budge. She tried again. Not even a hint of movement. Through it she could see the dark outline of the earth drop sharply away. Even if she broke the window and jumped, she'd probably break a leg—at least.

She circled the locked bedroom, searching for something sharp or heavy or lethal to use for a weapon. What could she do, charge at Mr. Upman and his gun, swinging a lamp or a bureau drawer? Try to slice him with the fragile sand dollar? She circled the room again. This was worse than the elevator feeling. The shadows in the room felt too distinct, too overdefined to make sense, oppressive. She paced, wall to wall, corner to corner.

Either stop this, she told herself, *or you'll soon be doing a scene from "The Yellow Wallpaper."*

She stood in the middle of the bedroom, swallowed, breathed steadily, and turned in a slow circle, counting to twenty by thousands, letting her mind relax as much as possible, allowing it to see and surmise without her interference.

She moved closer to two of the more familiar drawings. One was a heavy charcoal of two women in sarongs, unsigned but with a South Sea Gauguinish look to it. The other was a Toulouse-Lautrec, no doubt about it, a penciled original of high-kicking dancers.

Helma removed the South Sea women from the wall and carefully turned it over. "Paul Gauguin," it read on the back, "[1891?]"

She peeled back the paper backing and then used the sand dollar to pry off the inside matting. The drawing slid out of the glass frame and she gingerly held it in her hands, tracing the bold joyful strokes with her eyes, remembering it.

"I'm so sorry," she whispered.

Closing her eyes, grimacing at the sound, Helma tore the drawing into four ragged pieces.

Working quickly, she pulled the pillowcases off the bed pillows and draped them over one side of the lamp so they darkened the room but shone like a spotlight on the nightstand. In the spotlight she arranged the four torn pieces, crumpling one for dramatic effect, standing half a Tahitian woman against the lamp base so the ragged edge caught the full brunt of the light.

She stepped back into the shadows and surveyed her work. Her eyes moistened. It was terrible, a sacrilege.

It was perfect.

The lamp turned on and off at the light switch beside the door. Helma picked up the empty glass picture frame and turned off the light. The room went black, the only light visible from the view outside the window.

With one hand against the rough-textured wall, Helma inched away from the light switch. A picture wobbled beneath her fingers. She straightened it and stopped.

She should say something meaningful before she did this. She couldn't think of anything; it was too much like saying last words, anyway.

Instead, she took a deep breath, raised the picture frame above her head and threw it with all her might against the opposite wall.

It crashed and shattered, glass exploding in a satisfying clamor. Then Helma raised her voice, truly raised her voice. She screamed.

It began as a thin scream somewhere in her throat, and then it rose from a deeper place, deeper than her lungs, beneath her heart, a scream like a roar that was too big for the all-white bedroom, too big for Mr. Upman's house, almost too big for Helma.

She ran out of air and the scream subsided, thinned, and finally faded away. Helma smiled.

The door flung open. Light from the hallway picked out the bed, glinted on a glass picture frame.

"What's going on in here?"

Helma flattened herself against the wall, not daring to breathe.

"No tricks now, Miss Zukas," Mr. Upman said in a wickedly gentle voice. "I know you're in here. Are you sitting in the dark, thinking in your dim little mind that you can fool me? You couldn't fool a baby, Miss Wilhelmina Snoop Zukas. You're as transparent as a simpleton."

Mr. Upman stood in the doorway, backlit, his figure outlined like a shadow from a horror comic book. Helma glimpsed peripheral red flashes in the blackness of the room from holding her breath.

"I see you there, Helma. You may as well answer me."

He was lying. Helma didn't move.

Mr. Upman stepped into the room, the gun outstretched in his hand.

This is the moment, Helma thought, when the TV heroine jumps out and karate chops the handgun from the killer's hand. She held herself against the wall, thinking small, tiny, invisible. Mr. Upman took another step inside the bedroom. He held the gun in one hand, too skillfully at ease, and reached out to turn on the light.

The lamp on the nightstand came on, illuminating the tableau of the torn Gauguin like a shrine. The ragged edges shimmered, the bold strokes of the Tahitian woman's flowered sarong rose from the paper in disembodied beauty.

Mr. Upman stood only inches from Helma, transfixed. A growl of dismay rose in his throat. His gun wavered.

"You meddling bitch!" He took a step toward the destroyed drawing. "My God. What have you done?"

Helma jumped behind Mr. Upman and out the bedroom door. He whirled, but Helma was faster. She grabbed the doorknob and yanked the door closed behind her, slamming her elbow against the doorjamb.

Holding the doorknob and leaning all her weight into the hall, she felt frantically around the knob for the lock button. Mr. Upman's hands were already on the knob; it turned beneath her own hands like some live thing. Helma found the button and Mr. Upman wrenched the knob. With all her strength, Helma wrenched it back and pushed in the lock button. She ran down the hall toward the living room. The carpet was too slick. Running on it was like the running she did in dreams. Behind her, Mr. Upman kicked the door.

"Ruth!"

Ruth lay on the living room floor, still attached to the love seat. The telephone stretched on the floor beside her, off the hook.

"He didn't count on my being as strong as I look," Ruth said from the floor. "Dragging this thing wasn't so easy on the hands, though."

Ruth's wrists were bloodied from the plastic strip. A double crease of tracks marked the carpeting behind the love seat. On the floor lay the shattered crystal stag. The metallic clock lay in bits beside it. Metal balls spotted the carpet.

Helma picked up the phone. A familiar, soothing voice was droning from it.

"I already called," Ruth said. She stuck out her tongue. "Used my tongue. Reinforcements are on the way."

"Stop yammering and hurry it up!" Helma shouted into the phone.

A gunshot cracked from the bedroom. Helma dropped the phone and put her hand to her chest.

"He'll be out of there in no time," Ruth said. "Get out of here."

Helma tugged on the tough plastic that held Ruth's wrists. "I've got to find something to cut this. I can't leave you."

"The hell you can't. He's not going to hurt me. He knows I'm not going anywhere. All he cares about is saving his own tail. Get outside and wait for the police."

"No."

Ruth sat up and kicked Helma in the leg. "Get the hell out of here, you ass."

Down the hall, wood splintered.

"Get the hell out of here or I'll kill you myself."

Helma took a hesitant step toward the kitchen. A knife. She needed a knife.

"Go! Goddammit."

"Oh, Ruth."

"Go!"

Helma ran through the kitchen and out the wooden door that led into the garage. She flicked the light switch. Nothing happened. She felt her way to Upman's station wagon and jerked open the passenger door, throwing herself inside. Light. She needed light.

She frantically felt around the steering column and dashboard, searching for the headlight control, pushing and turning every knob and button she touched. The automatic garage door behind her rose, calmly whirring upward. The headlights came on and she jumped back out of the car.

She needed to see where the tools were: a hammer, a rake, an ax. He'd never reach his car to escape, she swore it.

A shot sounded from inside the house.

Ruth!

Helma stopped, her hand on a cabinet door.

Mr. Upman had shot Ruth! Helma was going back inside. She took a step toward the door.

Lights suddenly careened down the quiet street toward Mr. Upman's house. The police at last.

Helma turned and ran out of the garage into the middle of the driveway. She waved her arms as the car pulled in, tires squealing, slamming to a stop ten feet in front of her. The door opened.

"Hurry!" she shouted. "He's got a gun . . ."

The man getting out wasn't wearing a uniform. He held his arm close to his side. The passenger door opened and a second man stepped out. Casual, relaxed. Helma saw a glint of light from the street lamp reflect off something in his hand.

"Come on over here, ma'am. We're here to help," the driver said.

Helma hesitated. The other man raised his arm toward her and stepped into the light.

"Right this way, ma'am."

She knew that voice, recognized his modish haircut. It was the computer vendor from Destiny Computer Systems.

With a mighty leap, Helma threw herself out of the light in the driveway, around the corner of the garage. A piece of the wall splintered off above her head. She hadn't heard a shot. She dived into the ground and rolled beneath juniper shrubs, pressing herself flat into the cedar bark around the gnarled trunks.

The two men spoke quietly together, then more loudly. One of them said, "It'll go a lot easier for you, ma'am, if you come on out."

Helma didn't move. As she lay with her face pushed into cedar beauty bark, she was struck by unbearable grief. She saw it in her mind: Mr. Upman had shot Ruth. She'd left Ruth shackled to the love seat and run like a coward. She should have stayed with her. Whatever had happened to Ruth, she'd had to face it alone, just as Helma now would have to. She might as well stand up and get it over with.

Sirens. Their wails cried out as if from Helma herself. Sirens. The police were coming.

"Let's get the hell out of here," one of the men shouted.

"What about her?"

"You want to see your ass strung up? Forget her!"

The door between the kitchen and garage slammed and the footsteps hurried across the concrete floor.

"Speed it up!" the driver shouted to Mr. Upman.

The man on the passenger side opened the back door as the driver backed the car out of the driveway. Mr. Upman dived headfirst into the backseat. The tires screamed, the engine roared, and the car raced down the street with the back door still swinging open, its lights off. The car pulled out of the cul-de-sac and turned down the next street, shimmying as it took the corner. Lights came on in the houses nearby.

Helma ran to the curb. The red-and-blue lights of the police cars flashed, turning onto Mr. Upman's street. There were two police cars and more sirens wailed in the distance.

Helma waved her arms at the first police car. The officer rolled down his window.

"That way!" she pointed. "Down the next street to the left. There are three of them in a dark Pontiac. Call an ambulance! He shot my friend."

The officer nodded curtly. "Wait out here, ma'am. The officers behind us will take care of you. An ambulance is on the way." The driver was already on the police radio, calmly relaying code numbers and addresses.

Helma ran back to Mr. Upman's house as the other police cars pulled up. Sirens, lights. Shouts from neighbors.

"Ma'am. Stay outside," a voice called over a loud-speaker.

"Shut up!" Helma shouted and ran through the kitchen, calling, "Ruth?"

She stopped in the living room entry. The house was silent.

"Ruth?" she called again, softer.

The love seat blocked her view. Crimson stained the carpet around one end of the love seat. Ruth's foot protruded past the other end. Helma took a deep breath and stepped closer.

Blood seeped from Ruth's right shoulder, across her yellow sweatshirt. Her face was deathly pale, her breathing shallow. Helma knelt beside her.

"Ruth," she whispered. Ruth didn't move.

Two policemen and Chief Gallant entered the living room, their guns drawn.

"Helma," Chief Gallant said, reholstering his gun and taking her by the shoulders.

She nodded, trying to catch her breath.

"Ruth, he shot Ruth," Helma told him. "It was Mr. Upman. He left with the other men."

"Albert Upman," Chief Gallant said, not as a question and not sounding very surprised. He took off his jacket and laid it across Ruth. While he felt her throat for her pulse, one of the other officers knelt beside Ruth and cut the plastic strip that tied her bloodied wrists to the love seat. She groaned as he lowered her arms.

"Check the rest of the house," Chief Gallant said to the officers who'd materialized, weapons at the ready. Officer Lehman stood above them for a moment, looking down at Ruth before he continued through the house.

Then there were paramedics in the room. They gently pushed Helma out of the way and began working over Ruth, opening a case of silver and plastic instruments, listening to her heart, preparing oxygen, peering into her eyes. Competent, so self-assured that Helma's first feelings of panic subsided.

"Will she be all right?" Helma asked the paramedic who was cutting Ruth's sweatshirt at the neck.

"I can't say, ma'am."

"I'm sure with your experience you can," Helma said.

"Her vitals are good," he said. "We'll know more when we get her to the hospital."

"How did you and your friend end up here?" Chief Gallant asked as they stood watching the paramedics.

"Mr. Upman took us out on his sailboat today, and I believe he drugged us. He said he planned to slip us into the bay, but the weather was too nice."

"I beg your pardon?" Chief Gallant asked.

"The day was so pleasant that the bay was thick with boats," Helma explained. "Too many witnesses to just dump someone over the side of one's boat."

The paramedics made preparations to take Ruth to the ambulance. They strapped her on a gurney, too similar to the one in the morgue, a drip inserted into her arm, a mask over her face.

"I'd like to go with her," Helma said.

Chief Gallant laid his hand on her arm. "I'll take you to the hospital shortly. There are a few more questions I'd like to ask you."

"Can't they wait?"

"It'll only be a few moments, I promise."

"If I answer yours, will you answer mine?" she asked.

"It's a dea . . . an agreement," Chief Gallant said.

He led her away from the bloody carpet. "How were you able to get free?" he asked.

"He separated us," Helma told him. "It was a foolish move on his part. He bound Ruth to the love seat and locked me in a bedroom."

"Can you show me, please?"

Helma led him down the hall to the bedroom. The door hung only by its upper hinge, its lower half shattered.

"Is this how you escaped?" Chief Gallant asked.

"No, this is how he escaped. I was able to get out and lock him inside."

"I'd like to hear the details of that," the chief said and stepped into the bedroom. He stared at the shrouded lamp and torn drawing.

"I tore up a Gauguin," Helma explained. "To distract him."

Chief Gallant looked at her, a slight smile on his face. "Of course," he said.

He walked around the bedroom, jotting in his notebook without looking at what he wrote. He frowned at the Gauguin, then at the paintings on the wall. "It looks like Upman had a fairly extensive art collection."

"Ruth said they were originals," Helma told him.

Chief Gallant whistled through his teeth.

"Henry," he called.

One of the uniformed policemen appeared in the doorway.

"Yes, sir?"

"Make sure you get pictures of everything in this room."

"One of the men Mr. Upman escaped with has been to the library several times," Helma said. "He's been trying to sell the library a computer system."

"Did you ever see a demonstration of it?"

Helma shook her head. "None of the staff did. Only Mr. Upman."

Chief Gallant didn't say anything.

"Oh," Helma said. "Do you suspect there wasn't a computer system?"

"I'm sure there *is*, but I don't think that was the major business that was transpiring."

"Then what? For what reason have people died and been injured?"

"I think we'll have all the answers before the night is over. Why don't I take you to the hospital now?"

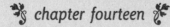
HELMA AND CHIEF GALLANT AT THE HOSPITAL

Hospitals weren't as institutional as they once were. Helma remembered sitting on a molded plastic chair as a child, in a vomit-yellow waiting room, while Helma's mother visited Helma's grandmother after her grandmother's stroke.

This waiting room was carpeted in soft gray, with pale cream walls and indirect lighting, furnished with deeply comfortable couches and chairs. Ruth was in surgery. The bullet had lodged near her upper spine.

"Would you like a cup of coffee?" Chief Gallant asked, handing Helma a Styrofoam cup.

"Thank you. That's very kind of you," Helma said as she took off the plastic lid.

She'd only tasted coffee once in her life, back in her first year of college. She'd found it far too bitter for her liking. She cautiously sipped the black liquid. It wasn't at all like she remembered. In fact, the smoky dark taste was almost pleasant.

Chief Gallant sat down next to her, rubbing the back of his neck. Above them in a corner of the room, a color television played without sound. Helma glanced around for a remote control to turn it off but she didn't see one.

"Are they still in surgery?" Helma asked.

Chief Gallant nodded.

They were the only people in the waiting room. Only nurses moved through the hospital corridors on their silent shoes, ministering to the mid-night needs of the patients.

"Now that Mr. Upman and his friends have been caught, shouldn't you be down at the station questioning them yourself?" Helma asked.

"I will later. We have very capable officers with them right now."

"Are they talking?" Helma asked.

"They're beginning to see the advantage. How did you know the word *vilké* meant she wolf?" he asked, pulling out his ever-present notebook.

"I already explained that. My roots are Lithuanian. I knew *vilkas* meant wolf—there was a nursery rhyme I knew once—and extrapolated from that. But you haven't explained why the word was used by Ernie Larsen."

Chief Gallant removed a stubby pencil from his shirt pocket. "Ernie Larsen's real name was Ernest Lesauskas."

"Oh. A Chicago Lithuanian. We guessed that. And his shoes were Rockports; he wasn't a transient, was he?"

Chief Gallant gazed up at the figures on the TV screen. "Not really."

"Then who was he?" Helma prodded.

"From what we've gathered, someone my niece would call a 'techno-nerd.' Brilliant, a college dropout, a real loner, with a sketchy past and an even sketchier means of support. For a while he wrote role-playing fantasies."

"What's that?"

"Creating worlds and characters for gamers. Like . . ."

"Mind games. Like Dungeons and Dragons."

"Similar. Then he opted to move closer to the fringe.

Computer hacking, computer espionage, first for one side, then the other. Last we knew he was playing amateur detective."

"Was he in costume when he came to the library? Playing a role?"

"I'd say so."

"Which side was he on?"

"Temporarily a marginal good guy, sleuthing for a computer firm that was losing chip technology."

"And he ended up dead in our library."

"Obviously the clues he left, and which you and Upman's pals found, were meant only for himself. If we'd known what the note said, since we already knew Ernie Larsen's true identity, we probably would have thought to check a Lithuanian dictionary."

"I did apologize for that," Helma reminded him. "If *I'd* known Ernie Larsen's true identity, I would have of course turned the note over to you."

"Would you have?"

"Certainly," Helma said. "But what about the organizational behavior book? How does that tie in? I looked all through it and couldn't find anything unusual, not a mark."

"Did you check beneath the security sticker in the back cover?"

"No, I didn't think of that. Clever, clever men. Disguises and tricks and games. There never was a plan to computerize the library system, was there? It was all computer espionage. The men from Destiny Computer Systems . . ."

"Which is actually a branch of World Technocracy," Chief Gallant added, "the leader in computer innovation."

" . . . smuggled the computer information through Mr. Upman, who put it under the security sticker in a boring book no one else would care to check out. Then what?"

"A borrower with a phony borrower's card checked out the book . . ."

"And gave the book to Calvin Whittington, the 'entrepreneur,' " Helma finished.

"Exactly. Covering their tracks all the way."

"And that's why Mr. Upman was so upset I was weeding the library collection without his permission—he was afraid I'd toss out his precious book?"

"That's right," Chief Gallant told her. He stretched and yawned, his arm brushing against Helma's.

"So when Mr. Upman botched everything by killing Ernie Larsen, Calvin Whittington came to town to do damage control?" she asked.

"And ended up dead himself."

Helma pulled her Styrofoam cup away from her mouth. Tooth marks partially ringed its rim and she turned it to the other side to sip her coffee. "You'd think they'd be finished in surgery by now, wouldn't you?"

He glanced at his watch. "It won't be long, I'm sure. They'll let us know as soon as they're done."

Somewhere a baby cried briefly, then was silent.

"What about Mr. Upman?" Helma asked. "Is he someone other than himself? He told me he was from Nevada."

"That's true."

"His father was a minister?"

Chief Gallant snorted. "Not hardly. His parents were quite the couple: gamblers and petty racketeers. Right now they're destitute, thanks to their son and probably the fine example they set for him, both of them living at the public's expense in a nursing home in Nevada. Upman raced through their money and ran up serious gambling debts of his own. Then he bought some art on phony credit and dropped out of sight."

"How do you know this?"

"We ran a check on everyone at the library. The information's still coming in."

"Even on me?" she asked.

He nodded.

"There wasn't much to my report, was there?"

"It was concise," he said.

Helma returned to the subject at hand. "And then Upman left Nevada and showed up here in Bellehaven?"

"After a while."

"He said his wife was a librarian."

"She was. She graduated from North Carolina. Your typical . . . well, from what we know, an innocent woman. I'd like to know how she got mixed up with him. In fact, it was through her that we made the connection with Upman. Her name was Alberta Upman."

"Albert*a*? That's a coinci . . ." Helma stopped. "No, it's not a coincidence at all, is it?"

The chief shook his head. "Upman was her maiden name."

"He assumed *her* identity and *her* career? That's diabolical! Did she really die of cancer?"

"A fall."

"How convenient. So our library has been directed by an impostor for four years. I can't believe it."

"He thought he found the ideal place to lie low. Small-town librarian. But old habits die hard." Now the chief stretched out his legs. Helma marveled at how far into the room they protruded. "How would you rate his library management skills?" he asked Helma.

"In light of this information, I feel vindicated for some of my earlier opinions."

Chief Gallant laughed.

"I suspect that when the art hanging on his walls and what we found in a locked storage room off his bedroom is appraised, we'll discover that he possessed a considerable fortune that could only appreciate in time."

"The art would call little attention to him. No flashy cars or wild living."

"Right. His only obvious indulgence was his sailboat,

which no one would raise an eyebrow over in this part of the country."

"This has been a strenuous investigation," Helma said.

"Some aspects of it have been more pleasant than others," Chief Gallant said, smiling at Helma.

Helma ducked her head.

They sat in silence. On the television above them, a family scene played just as silently: tearful hugs and smiles.

Helma closed her eyes. She might have dozed; she wasn't sure. The night did funny things with her sense of time. She opened her eyes and a doctor, still wearing his green scrubs, was standing in the waiting room, smiling.

"Well, we have good news," he said. "Your friend will have a period of recovery, but there's no permanent damage. No spinal damage."

"That's wonderful," Helma said. "When can I see her?"

"Tomorrow," the doctor told her. "She's in Recovery right now."

"Thanks, Ben," Chief Gallant said and shook the doctor's hand.

"It's a pleasure to be the bearer of good news," the doctor told them.

"I'll take you home," Chief Gallant told Helma. "Try to get a little sleep and come back tomorrow. You might call your mother in the morning, too."

"My mother!" Helma said. "Oh, Faulkner. I forgot. She was expecting me for dinner this afternoon—yesterday afternoon I guess it is now."

"She phoned me when you didn't show up. That sped up our investigation considerably, I can assure you. But don't worry. One of my men contacted her once we knew you were all right. She knows a little of what happened, but I think she's very curious."

"I'm sure," Helma replied.

* * *

"You must not be coming into work, dressed like that," Patrice said.

"Helma!" Eve cried. She ducked beneath the counter and hugged Helma. "You're all right! There are all kinds of stories going around. Are they true?"

"I'm not sure," Helma said. "What are they?"

Eve smelled like baby powder and chocolate. She ticked off her fingers. "That our leader is actually a thief, a spy, and a *murderer*. And he tried to murder you." Eve's face fell. "And that he shot your friend. Will she be OK?"

"I think so. I'm going to visit her in a few minutes."

"Have you notified anyone you're taking the day off?" Patrice asked.

"I'll leave a note on Mr. Upman's desk," Helma told her.

Eve giggled and belatedly covered her mouth. Patrice sucked in her cheeks.

"There's nothing humorous about this situation." Patrice's voice rose. "Nothing. I . . . we, that is, trusted that man, that charlatan."

Patrice's face crumpled as if she were about to cry. They all stared at her. Eve patted her shoulder.

"*I* never did," George Melville said, balancing an overfull mug of coffee. "I had a suspicion from Day One."

"Hindsight, hindsight," Eve sang out.

"So that ends our little foray into the twentieth century world of computerized card catalogs, I guess," he added.

"It was a joke from the beginning," Patrice said. "He never meant it. It wouldn't have worked, even if he had."

"I don't know," Helma said. "Maybe if we were all involved in the selection of a system . . ."

"Are you inciting cooperation, Helma?"

"I've heard it's worked in other institutions."

Helma glanced up at the clock over the circulation

desk. It was nearly ten, time for the library to open and time for hospital visiting hours.

She had one hand on the library door when Eve caught up with her. "Helma," Eve said breathlessly. "I didn't want to ask you in front of Patrice, but you know Polly at the police department? She said that . . . well, that Chief Gallant spent the night with you instead of at the police station with the criminals."

Helma felt an unaccustomed rising of blood to her cheeks. "I can assure you, that's completely untrue," Helma told her. "He took me to the hospital while Ruth had surgery and asked questions, all in the line of official police business. It was. Completely. Really. I assure you."

Eve grinned and squeezed Helma's arm. "I think he's cute, don't you?"

"I hadn't noticed," Helma told her.

Helma stood at Ruth's door for a moment, looking in at the pale, supine Ruth, dressed in pastel hospital blue. The head of Ruth's bed was raised and her right side wore a bulk of bandages. A drain led from the bandages and a drip was positioned beside her bed, with a tube snaking down into the back of Ruth's hand. Ruth had been effectively shorn of her flamboyance; she even looked smaller. Only her hair remained determinedly out of control.

"Oh fun," Ruth said when she saw Helma.

"Isn't it though?" Helma said. "Here are the customary hospital gifts." She held up a potted gloxinia and a box of chocolates.

"Open the chocolates please, dear woman. Let's pig out."

"Are you allowed?"

Ruth winced as she turned farther toward Helma. "I most certainly am allowed," she said. "Wounded but recovering gunshot victims are treated with the utmost kindness around here."

"Has the chief been in to see you yet?"

"At the crack of dawn. Wanted to hear all the grisly criminal details. I understand Upman and his cronies are cooling off in the hoosegow. He was skipping the country after this little job. I guess he can't get over the injustice of having all his careful plans trashed."

Ruth picked up a chocolate with her left hand, scraped away the chocolate at the bottom until it showed a pink center, put it back, and did the same to another; it had a white center. She popped it in her mouth. "That'll be one trial it'll be a pleasure to attend. Maybe they'll let him put together a little library when they send him up."

"You're very lucky he didn't kill you," Helma said around a chocolate with a maple center.

"Ain't I though? What a prick. How did you get mixed up with such a slimeball?"

"I hardly did that."

Ruth winked at Helma. "You were a gutsy lady, sneaking out of the bedroom and locking him in."

Helma felt her face warming for the second time. "*You* dragged the love seat to the phone, and then had to face Mr. Upman alone."

"OK, so we were both gutsy ladies. Chief Shining Armor said Upman—or whatever his real name is— can't stop talking. He and Whittington quarreled after the job with me was botched. Old Uppie likes to end quarrels permanently, I guess."

"Mmm."

Ruth looked Helma up and down. "You're dressed rather casually for a workday."

"I took the day off."

"No!"

"The library's in a turmoil anyway."

"I can imagine. They'll need a new director. You'd be perfect. Easy shoes to fill."

"It will be a while before any decisions are made."

"You seem relaxed," Ruth said. She laid her head

back against her pillow. Chocolate stained her lower lip.

"The element of danger has been removed," Helma reminded her.

"In fact, I'd say you look quite happy for all that's taken place around here lately. You might even say you look like you've been enjoying yourself."

Ruth's eyes closed for a long moment.

"You're tired, Ruth," Helma said. "I've been here too long. I'll come back tomorrow."

Ruth sighed and drowsily said, "Can you bring my oils? All the reds. I've got to finish that painting."

Helma put the cover back on the box of chocolates and set them beside the gloxinia. "I'm leaving now, Ruth," she whispered. "You rest and I'll see you tomorrow."

Ruth barely nodded; her eyes didn't open. Helma checked the drip to be sure there was plenty of solution in the collapsible hanging bag, then left the room.

Helma drove slowly along the boulevard. The islands were invisible, socked in behind misty gray clouds that touched the water and moved across the bay toward Bellehaven. She pulled into the first parking area that faced the water and turned off the engine. A young couple sat in the car next to her, their arms around one another, earnestly intent on each other, oblivious to anyone else.

Helma slipped off her shoes and socks and pulled her bare feet onto the seat beside her. She wiggled her toes, thinking about the red nail polish Ruth wore. Her own feet were shaped rather nicely, as feet went. Feet were definitely not the body's most attractive feature.

A lone sailboat tacked into the rising wind on the bay. Helma watched its solitary passage as the misty clouds reached shore and a light rain began to fall against her windshield.